Darkness at the Edge of Town

a ghostly tale of family ties and madness

ESSENTIAL PROSE SERIES 195

Canada Council **Conseil des Arts**
for the Arts **du Canada**

ONTARIO ARTS COUNCIL
CONSEIL DES ARTS DE L'ONTARIO

an Ontario government agency
un organisme du gouvernement de l'Ontario

Canada

Guernica Editions Inc. acknowledges the support of the Canada Council
for the Arts and the Ontario Arts Council. The Ontario Arts Council
is an agency of the Government of Ontario.

We acknowledge the financial support of the Government of Canada.

Darkness at the Edge of Town

*a ghostly tale of family ties
and madness*

STAN ROGAL

GUERNICA
EDITIONS
TORONTO • CHICAGO • BUFFALO • LANCASTER (U.K.)
2022

Copyright © 2022, Stan Rogal and Guernica Editions Inc.
All rights reserved. The use of any part of this publication,
reproduced, transmitted in any form or by any means,
electronic, mechanical, photocopying, recording
or otherwise stored in a retrieval system, without the prior consent
of the publisher is an infringement of the copyright law.

Guernica Founder: Antonio D'Alfonso

Michael Mirolla, general editor
Sonia di Placido, editor
David Moratto, interior and cover design
Guernica Editions Inc.
287 Templemead Drive, Hamilton, ON L8W 2W4
2250 Military Road, Tonawanda, N.Y. 14150-6000 U.S.A.
www.guernicaeditions.com

Distributors:
Independent Publishers Group (IPG)
600 North Pulaski Road, Chicago IL 60624
University of Toronto Press Distribution (UTP)
5201 Dufferin Street, Toronto (ON), Canada M3H 5T8
Gazelle Book Services, White Cross Mills
High Town, Lancaster LA1 4XS U.K.

First edition.
Printed in Canada.

Legal Deposit—First Quarter
Library of Congress Catalog Card Number: 2021946926
Library and Archives Canada Cataloguing in Publication
Title: Darkness at the edge of town : (a ghostly tale of family ties and
madness) / Stan Rogal.
Names: Rogal, Stan, 1950- author.
Series: Essential prose series ; 191.
Description: Series statement: Essential prose series ; 191.
Identifiers: Canadiana (print) 20210314761
| Canadiana (ebook) 20210314788 | ISBN 9781771836975 (softcover)
| ISBN 9781771836982 (EPUB)
Classification: LCC PS8585.O391 D37 2022 | DDC C813/.54—dc23

Dedicated to my mom—born a prairie girl—
who had a story or two herself, to tell

"It takes two to make an accident."
  —F. Scott Fitzgerald, *The Great Gatsby*

"A man turns his back on his family, he just ain't no good."
  —Bruce Springsteen, "Highway Patrolman"

"As if there could possibly be true stories; things happen one way and we tell them in the opposite sense."
  —Jean-Paul Sartre, *Nausea*

1.

Welcome to Weyburn, Saskatchewan, largest inland grain gathering point in Canada. Summer, 2017

The house isn't grand; it's functional. Comfy/cosy/homey. Located on a quiet suburban cul-de-sac within a loose knit of neighbourly neighbours. Three-bedroom rancher, full bath, open-concept living/dining room combination, up-dated kitchen with *faux* chrome appliances. Mud room at rear of house, complete with stacked clothes washer/dryer unit. One small bedroom used as a catch-all and office space; one medium-sized bedroom for the kids—four-year-old Ben junior and two-year-old daughter Casey sharing a bunk bed—a larger master bedroom with en suite. Everything painted either off-white or soothing pastels. Furniture straight out of the Ikea catalogue with a few select pieces picked from the sales department at Home Depot. Front yard has a postage-stamp lawn divided by a concrete walkway. Decorative stacked red bricks delineate several compact flower and shrub beds. There's the usual mix of Canadian Tire plaster or plastic garden ornaments: forest animals, birds, gnomes, semi-naked wood nymphs. Decent-sized backyard with swing set and slide, pressure-treated wood deck enclosed in a gazebo of canvas with nylon mosquito netting, a Weber gas BBQ to one side, a huge garage with automatic folding door that serves as storage area for every type of wheeled recreational vehicle as well as sports equipment and gym accessories: barbells, weights, mats, medicine ball, Ab roller wheel, skipping rope, Bowflex machine. The grey cinder block structure also functions as a workshop: steel bench, metal display racks of tools, labeled bins of nails, screws, nuts, bolts, a plastic pail of soiled, oily rags, rolls of duct tape.

Everything neat and tidy; a place for everything and everything in its place. Blame Ben, who—while not willing to admit subscribing to the worn adage that cleanliness is next to godliness—prefers order to disorder.

His wife Beth, not so much. Likes to say she strives for organized clutter, 'strives' being the operative word.

It's late evening. The kids are asleep. The A/C hums. The soiled remains of dinner decorate the dining table: dirty cutlery, stained dishes, ravaged pork rib bones, crumpled paper napkins smeared in grease and BBQ sauce. Empty beer bottles leave a trail into the living room. Ben lounges on the couch with a goofy Cheshire cat toothy grin nailed on his wide face. Between his loose-parted knees he dangles a Canada Dry Ginger Ale bottle by the neck. The switch from beer was made a couple hours ago. He wears his official police uniform, still on-duty. His black hair's cropped close to the scalp and his short sleeve shirt strains at the button-holes to contain his broad chest. Not a bit of bulge on him. He's built solid as an oak tree; developed muscular arms from hours pumping iron and performing endless reps of push-ups and chins in the garage.

What one might admirably call the proverbial six-foot brick shit house.

The music of Bruce Springsteen blasts through compact Bose stereo speakers: *Glory Days.* Ray and Beth dance a slow sloppy jive in the middle of the parquet floor. Ray gives her a twirl. Stretched at arm's length, held by fingertips, she tosses her head backwards so that her hair hangs down, then laughs, spins back toward him, and nestles in his chest.

Ben rocks his head to the tune and hums along. He's interrupted by his cell. The ringtone is Wagner's, *Ride of the Valkyries,* straight off the movie soundtrack, "Apocalypse Now."

"Crap," he says, and answers. "Yeah?" He flaps the fingers of one hand toward the pair on the dance floor, *yakkity-yak*. They barely acknowledge. He pockets the cell.

"Whassup?" Beth asks. Her words carry a slight throaty slur from the effects of the alcohol.

"Same ol' same ol'. Got a problem at the precinct only I can handle. Needs my official John Hancock, apparently. We'll see."

Ray puts on a low southern drawl. "What happens, son, when you acquire a position of authority and responsibility in this here town."

"Yeah. Me and the dog catcher. Highly respected." He gets to his feet and dons his hat. "Gonna take me twenty/thirty minutes tops to be back. You still be here?"

"Not likely. Gotta hit the road myself. Gettin' late. Just finish my beer." He waves his bottle in the air.

"You can crash here if you want. Couch is a fold-out."

"Not necessary, but thanks."

"Sure. Anyhow, now you know where we are, don't be a stranger. Or maybe we can set up a once-a-week. You said you don't have a phone, right, cell or otherwise?" Ben shakes his head, no, along with Ray and Beth. They all laugh. It's become an inside joke already, the subject having been flogged to death during the evening's early conversation, as: How can you exist in the 21st century without owning a cell?

"You got a milk calendar, anyway, yeah?" Ben nods his head, yes, like he's talking to an infant. "Circle Sunday nights."

Ray circles the air with a finger and dots it for emphasis.

"Okay, glad we got that settled. It's good to see you, Ray. Truly. Welcome back. We'll continue catching up another time. Maybe get you out for a few hours fishing." He kisses Beth tenderly on the lips.

"Leave this." He motions to the mess. "I'll clean up when I get home. No worries." He gives a relaxed half-salute to the pair, lifts his holster from a hook and hustles out the front door.

"Whee! I haven't drank this much in years," Beth says. Her voice is all warm and creamy. "Or is it 'drunk?' *I'm* drunk. Ha! It's kinda nice. Being tipsy. Been a while. I almost forgot." She raises her chin and locks eyes with Ray. The two are engaged in a sort of loose-armed embrace, their bodies set just close enough together you could barely slip a cigarette paper between them. "You look good, mister. Fit. Muscular. Not as full-out muscular as Ben. More like a wrapped-tight coil of razor wire, all sharp angles, edges and points. You could cut a person, really, if you weren't careful, just by casually turning your head. Don't get me wrong, it suits you. I like it. The time away hasn't hurt you any, looks wise, anyway. Maybe helped. Ya used to be skinny." She sucks a deep breath into her lungs and her breasts swell against his rib cage. "You gonna kiss me now, or what? Little brother's not watching." She pops her lips and grins mischievously.

"Hey. How'd the little boy mouse meet the little girl mouse? Remember?"

She crawls her hands around Ray's neck and hauls herself up on tippy toes. She's about five-foot-two in bare feet. Ray has a good eight or nine inches on her in motorcycle boots.

"I kissed you when I showed earlier."

"A peck. A peck on the cheek. Sisterly. I think you owe me at least one real kiss, after all."

"Uh-huh? How do you figure?"

"You practically left me standing at the altar, bastard."

"I think that's an exaggeration of what was our relationship at the time."

"Not to me. I had it all planned out. Down to the dress, the cake, even the flowers on the table. Black-eyed Susans mixed with baby's breath."

"Impressive. You were, what? All of eighteen?"

"So?"

"So? So, you were better off waiting. You got Ben. Lucky girl. Nice home, nice family. Count your blessings."

"Yeah, got an automatic dishwasher, microwave oven and everything. All the modern conveniences." She huffs. "One lousy kiss is all I'm asking. What are ya, scared?"

"Should I be?"

"Yer damn right," she says with a snarl. "Now be a good boy and pucker up." She half-shuts her eyes, steps her feet on top of his boots and presses her body into his. Ray bends his head to meet hers and they kiss, heavy and full. Beth tries to slip him the tongue and he peels her away by the shoulders. She shoots him a dirty grin. "Mm, sweet. Wasn't so hard now, was it? The kiss, I mean. Unlike something else

I might mention." She laughs and eyeballs his crotch. "Which *is* hard, yeah? Nice to know you haven't changed, Ray."

"And your high beams are drilling holes through your summer frock, so let's consider us even. And done."

"I'm wet, too, if it matters." The words are spoken like a challenge. She pulls provocatively at her lower lip and gazes at him through slit eyes.

"I didn't come here tonight to try and cause trouble."

He drains his beer, keeping his free arm extended, Beth attached and somewhat constrained at the outermost end.

"Ha! Don't make me laugh. You don't need to try to cause trouble, Ray. It follows you around like a trained dog. You don't even need to whistle and it's there." She slaps and pushes his hand off her shoulder and stumbles backward. She moves flat-footed, her arms floppy. "You mean to say you never noticed? C'mon! You walk into a department store and things fall off the shelves and smash on the floor for no obvious reason. Crash, bang! You enter a bar, fights break out. Wham, bam! Blood and black eyes and broken bones everywhere. You walk down a sidewalk, young girls suffer moist panties and broken hearts. Babies cry. Mothers weep. Oh my God!" She runs her hands up the back of her neck, into her scalp. "You shake your hair out on a main street of Weyburn and you cause a freaking typhoon in China." She scratches the top of her forehead and smirks. "I mean ... what was that all about, huh? That grand entrance? Like something out of the movies. Marlon Brando in *The Wild One* or whatever." She puts on a meek voice. "What are you rebelling against, son?" Then a different voice, harsher, snarkier. "I don't know, mister, what have you got?" She smacks her lips. "Isn't that it? The way it goes. The hokey dialogue."

"I don't know Beth." He adds his empty bottle alongside others on the coffee table. "That movie was a lifetime ago."

"Yeah? Tell me about it. Ben plays it, like, three or four times a year, faithfully. He owns his very own copy. Not sure why. Says it serves as a reminder. I ask, a reminder of what, honey? Raising hell and causing all kinds of trouble? That was never you. He just throws his hands in the air and says he isn't sure. Perfect. Well, Ben, *thankyouverymuch*. And since he's got nothing more to say on the subject, we settle on the couch, drink beer, eat buttered popcorn and watch the film. Again." She tugs at a strand of straight brown hair and tucks it behind an ear. "I was trying to make a point. What was I saying?" She snaps her fingers rapidly at Ray.

"I don't know Beth. You're drunk. Something about an entrance."

"Yeah, what was with that, huh? You showing up out of the blue a week ago, after ... what? Seven years? Seven god-damn years. Like in the fairy tales. And in you come, slung pretty-as-you-please on the seat of a classic, souped-up, cherry-red Triumph motorcycle. Wowie-zowie!"

She uses a hand to mimic gunning the engine. She duplicates the sound with a hoarse: *vroom, vroom*.

"You're getting loud, Beth. The kids."

"Oh, yeah, the kids." She pulls a guilty face and places a fingertip to her lips, then lets out a belly laugh. "Nice try. Just 'cause you're embarrassed. The kids are fine, Ray. The kids are all right, yeah?" She semi-sings the words. More a warble. "The Kids are all right. Old song. The Who, remember? Eh? No? Anyway, they're zonked out dead to the world, don't concern yourself. And even if they do wake up, so what? Nothin' to see here, right? Please keep back of the yellow

7

tape. Fine, fine." She bites her lower lip. "Let's get back to you." She twirls a finger, points the tip at him, and drives it forward. "Straight up Government Road. Like you own the goddamn place. Middle of the afternoon, sun blazing overhead. Everyone else on the road pulls over and parks. They don't know what to make of it. It's like a phenomenon. They don't know what else to do. They don't know whether to shit or wind their watches. Pedestrians stop in mid-stride. Shoppers lean into windows to catch a glimpse. Each and every one disconnects from their electronic devices to fully appreciate the scene. Holy traffic stopper, Batman! Even birds land and crowd the electric power lines for a peek. What the ...? Who is this guy?" She squeezes the brakes hard and grits her teeth. "Eeeeeee! You screech to a halt in the centre of the intersection. The bike fishtails. You sit there frozen like a park statue. White T-shirt, black denim pants, black leather boots, sunglasses, freaking tattoos on your biceps. The whole bit, wham bam! Almost expect to hear *The Ballad of Easy Rider* playing in the background." Beth goes all Hollywood dramatic, dropping her jaw and widening her eyes. "That's when you stripped the elastic band from your hair and gave your thick, curly, raven locks an energetic shake. Yikes! You might've been shooting a commercial for Old Spice or Axe or something. Everything suddenly went slo-mo. Everyone gasped in unison. It was fucking unbelievable."

"You were there? You witnessed it?"

"Yeah, as it so happens, I did. I was working a shift at the diner. Had a clear shot through the picture window of the entire mad scene. Not that it mattered. Even folks who weren't there claim they were. It was a clear case of mass hysteria that affected everyone in the town, whether near or far. The vision of that entrance—of *you*—was pasted on people's brains equally. It was like they'd witnessed the figure of Jesus Christ, or the holy Virgin Mary burn itself into the blue brick wall of a Walmart store. Believe me, in that instant, you attained the status of demi-god; an image firmly entrenched in the psyche of the populace, one-part awe, three parts fear."

"Fear? Fear of what?"

"The unknown, sweets, what else? Whether you dropped out of the sky from heaven or crawled out from the depths of hell, didn't matter. 'Course, I knew it was you right away. Who else? Ben, too. He likely crossed himself in the patrol car."

"I think you're making too much of it. I was just trying to get my bearings, pick out familiar landmarks. The place has changed."

"Yeah. In some ways, in others, not so much." She rolls her head and inhales through her nose. "I'm in the mood for a scotch. You want one? Join me? Good stuff! Single malt. Was a gift from someone for something. Christmas, probably. Been sitting there, waiting."

"Sure. A short one, why not?"

Beth skips over to a white modular entertainment unit, squats on the flats of her feet, opens a cupboard door and produces a bottle and two glasses. She pours. The music continues to play. John Anderson singing something about straight tequila nights and a broken heart.

"Ice? Water?"

"Neat is good."

"Neat *is* good." Beth dances the drinks over and they clink glasses.

"People get strange ideas. They see what they want to see, hear what they want to hear, believe what they want to believe. I can't help that."

"No need to go all dark and philosophical on me, Ray. Like I give a flying fuck what people think." She shrugs. "The only real question is: What took you so long to get in touch with us? Ben and me. I mean, what the hell?"

"I wanted to get myself set up. Find a place. Didn't want you to think you needed to take care of me."

"Uh-huh. I see." She runs a tongue tip across her lips. "I hear you're livin' with that crazy Indian woman in her run-down trailer in the middle of nowhere."

Beth can't help but shake the bee jar to attempt a reaction. Ray refuses to bite. "She's Cree and she has a name—Tantoo Morningstar."

"Giving her some sort of official designation doesn't change the fact she's crazy. And stinks to high heaven."

"Maybe not." Ray considers pursuing the argument and doesn't. Beth has the ball, let her run with it.

"I'm just sayin'." Beth crinkles her nose and puckers her lips. "Besides, how'd you manage to shack up with her?"

"We're not shacked up. We met at the Detour. She was there sellin' bead bracelets and necklaces and whatnot. We talked." He bobs his head. "Well, *I* talked. I somehow mentioned I needed a place to stay, she *communicated* ..."—he flutters his fingers in the air—"... she had an extra room she could rent me cheap. That was it."

"Uh-huh. I see. Right." Beth knocks back the scotch, runs an index finger around the inside of the glass and sticks the finger in her mouth. "Yum. And I'm supposed to believe that because ..."

"Believe what you want, Beth."

"She's gotta be like what: twenty, twenty-five years older than you. You can't really be banging her, can you? I mean, I'd think the smell, alone ..."

Ray steps forward and holds a flat palm in front of her face: talk to the hand.

"Enough, okay? Before you say something ... what? Inappropriate."

Beth swats at the hand, like a fly, and Ray retracts it. She mimes zipping her lips shut, turning a lock and throwing away the key. She brushes her hands clean.

"Satisfied?" she says.

"I'm gonna vamoose. You look fine, Beth, really. Thanks for the dinner. It was excellent. We'll have to do it again sometime."

He hands her his empty glass. She scrunches her eyes, sucks in her cheeks and squeezes her lips to a point.

"Remember what we used to call this face?"

"Cat's ass."

"Uh-huh." She relaxes. "Cat's ass. Meow. Just go, Ray. You're lousy at compliments and even worse at goodbyes."

"You're probably right."

Ray slips his arms into a light denim jacket and hunches out of the house. Beth walks to the living room window, watches him start the Triumph, kick out the driveway, motor up the road and evaporate into the dust around a curve. She raises a middle finger into the air and uses the tip to rub the bridge of her nose.

Fuck you, Ray, she mumbles. *Fuck you and the horse you rode in on.*

2.

Ben scrambles eggs as Beth empties the dishwasher. The kitchen's filled with aromas of fresh brewed coffee and buttered toast. The kids are at the dining room table. Ben junior busy with a colouring book; Casey strapped into a highchair stabbing her oatmeal with a plastic spoon.

"Gonna be another scorcher," Ben says, squinting out the window.

"It's middle of August. What do you expect?"

"I guess. Seems hotter for some reason."

"That's why God invented A/C." Beth smiles and gives Ben's arm a squeeze.

"They say maybe a storm sometime this afternoon."

"I heard. One of those two-minute deluges, *pock-pock-pock*. Wind, thick black roiling clouds, thunder, lightning, then *poof*, gone. Hardly time to open an umbrella never mind quench your thirst or douse the crops. I'm taking the kids to the water park anyway. It'll be part of the soak." She rattles cutlery into a drawer. "Why do you think he's come back, huh? Ray, I'm talking about. I mean, why now?"

"He must've read the latest propaganda in the local tourist guides. *Welcome to the opportunity city*!"

"Haha, right."

Ben shrugs. "Ask me why he left."

"Are you kidding? A million good solid reasons I can think of off the top of my head. Not the least of which, he could never sit still. Classic case of ants in the pants. Part and parcel with being a Virgo, I'd say. They get bored and frustrated stuck doing the same mundane chores over and over. Always restless, always looking for something, always ... I don't know ... *expecting* something, though never sure what. Typical Type A personality: single-minded, judgmental and critical of others."

"I always heard Virgos were healers who had a talent for fixing things."

"That's the flip side of the same coin: your typical Jekyll and Hyde situation. The exact same attributes that make one person a saint make another a sinner. It's all a matter of degree."

"Hmm."

"You know Ray went from shit job to shit job 'til no one would hire him anymore, yeah? Kept pissing people off. One thing, whatever it was he was looking for, it sure as hell wasn't in *Wey*-burn. It was just a matter of time before he took off for greener pastures. What I took to be forever."

"Greener pastures, right. To go where, really? To do what?"

Beth grunts, stacks plates in the cupboard and suddenly chuckles to herself.

"What? Tell me." Ben reduces the heat under the eggs.

"I just recalled ..."

"What?"

"There was that business with Suzanne Leask, yeah? Claimed Ray got her preggers. That riled the family. Didn't her brother lose a few teeth and almost an ear trying to defend her so-called honour?"

"Yeah. Turned out to be more in her head than in her belly."

"Doesn't mean Ray didn't ... you know ..."—Beth jams an index finger in and out of a circle formed by her other hand—"... do the nasty with her. I believe he must've had sex with every eligible—and not so eligible—girl in town. And some of their mothers. The most annoying part was, he didn't have to do a goddamn thing. He had a sort of natural animal magnetism, a certain energy about him that made women just want to drop their laundry and open their legs. Like they had no choice in the matter. Huh." She wipes a pot dry with a tea towel and bangs it onto a shelf. For someone with a relatively compact frame, she tends to create a huge racket doing the simplest chores. "Hey! What's the difference between a light bulb and a pregnant woman?" She allows barely a pause. "You can unscrew a light bulb." She snorts. "Pretty hilarious. Anyway, it was bound to catch up with him sooner or later. Either a baby or a bullet." She smacks her forehead with the heel of a hand. "*Pow!* Wake up call." She steps to the sink, hoists a plastic bag of frozen food and presents it to Ben. "I pulled chicken thighs out of the freezer for dinner, okay?"

"Sure. I'll toss them on the BBQ with corn on the cob." He gives the eggs a stir. "As I recall—and correct me if I'm wrong—you were a part of that fallen group, yeah? Dropping laundry, *et cetera, et cetera* ... and pined almost a full two years after he was gone, *boo-hoo, boo-hoo.*"

"Don't be mean." She swats Ben with the frozen chicken and he responds accordingly, with a slight flinch and a playful *ouch*. "And look who's calling the kettle black. As I recall, mister, you weren't too happy about his leaving and went through your own period of private personal hell."

"Yeah, I guess that's true. Over now, though."

"Uh-huh. Anyway, I never said he couldn't be somehow charming and sweet, in his own narcissistic way. What do they call it? Boyish innocence. Right. Butter wouldn't melt in his mouth. When he wanted something, that is, which was often. You know better than anyone. He crashed up your first car, right? Drunk and disorderly. Likely getting a blowjob in the front seat by some girl you were attracted to, or worse, dating, and you let it go. Whatever he did—to you or anyone—no matter how bad or hurtful, you always forgave him."

"He's my brother."

"Sure. And family's family. Still."

"And what about you? Seeing him now? Does it bring back fond and precious memories or what?"

"No need to worry yourself, Ben, honey. I got the right brother. I know that. I'm happy. I love our kids. Ray's here today, gone tomorrow. You're my rock." She kisses him on the side of the mouth. "And *why-ever* he's returned after seven long years, I know I'm not the attraction. But it's something."

Ben dishes the eggs onto plates with a wooden spoon. "He's got a birthday coming up in two weeks. He'll turn twenty-nine."

"Closing in on thirty. You think maybe that's it? I mean, I have a tough time thinking of Ray as nostalgic, but maybe he's feeling his age, yeah? And maybe wants to touch base with his roots? I don't know. Stranger things happen, I suppose."

"Yeah, maybe. Of course, our mother disappeared shortly after she turned twenty-nine. Do you think that's a coincidence?"

"Huh. Disappeared? I thought she drowned."

"They say she drowned. They found her shoes, covered by a neatly folded blouse, by the riverbank, but they never found her body. Ray and I used to make up stories about her. About how she was still alive and living somewhere else. We'd even go so far as to imagine her in adventurous situations sometimes: climbing mountains or crossing deserts and confronting some kind of danger or whatever. That sort of thing. Kid stuff. Of course, the exercise lost its shine after a while—*tempus fugit*, and so on—and we believed like everyone else that she was dead. At least, I did."

"Ray didn't?"

"He said he did, though every so often—especially after one too many drinks—he'd bring up the subject again and say, hey, do you think mom might be sittin' on a big boat somewhere on the ocean right this moment, sippin' a martini and wonderin' how we're doin' and what we're up to? He'd catch himself almost immediately and say he was joking, but he'd have that faraway look in his eyes that made me wonder."

"Uh-huh. I've seen that look." She shrugs. "Well, I'm gonna give Ben junior his eggs. I'm sure we'll know soon enough. I don't expect Ray to be around for the winter, if you know what I mean."

"Yeah. I just hope it's nothing crazy." Ben shovels scrambled eggs onto toast, adds ketchup for a sandwich, and eats standing. "Or, who knows, maybe he's come back to stay. Settle down. Maybe he's had his fill of the outside world. That'd be nice, huh?"

"Ha! Yeah, when pigs fly." Beth carries eggs and coffee over to the table. She sets the breakfast in front of Ben junior. He digs in. She sips her coffee. "Maybe he's also running from the law and needs a place to lay low for a spell." She hears Ben tap the wooden spoon on the stove. "I hate to mention, hon, though it wouldn't surprise me. Anyway, you probably have to ask if you want to know. He's never been much for volunteering information."

"I'll do that. Meanwhile, you need me to pick up anything in town, or ...?"

"I'll get groceries. You might want to pick up more beer. We did a job last night."

"You mean you and Ray did a job. I was on-call."

"That's what I said, *we* did a job. And who knows, he might just turn up again tonight, or anytime unannounced for that matter, so we might as well be prepared. Only, you can keep him company this time." She pats her hands down her sides. "Beer goes right to my hips. Blame my German heritage."

Beth liked to tell anyone with half an interest, her background was German, Hungarian and Polish, plus any other fool either brave or horny enough to jump the fence, making her one hundred percent pure-bred Canadian stock.

"You look great."

"You mean for having two kids?"

"I mean anytime. You look terrific."

"You're sweet even if you are a liar."

The pair kiss. Ben says his good-byes to the kids and leaves through the front door. Beth goes to the hall mirror and gives herself a study. She rocks her head and purses her lips. Not too bad, she thinks, all things considered. She twists her body slightly. Butt's still firm and the breasts are in fine shape. She cups and bounces them, then pinches at her tummy. Maybe I could stand to lose a few pounds of spare tire. An hour or two a day on the treadmill should take care of that, no problem. Watch what I eat, don't snack. Lay off the beer, sort of. Otherwise, pretty damned okay, I'd say. Definitely worth the whistle, you bet.

3.

Late morning, middle of nowhere, sun beating down on the bleak terrain. Off to one side of the dirt road, a lone camper trailer sits atop a foundation of loose cinder blocks and boards, its only connection to civilization being a single electric umbilical cord running from a wooden pole pinned at the road's edge.

Tantoo sits in tattered skirts cross-legged on the ground. A thin, colourful, woven blanket beneath her. She guides a needle and thread through several beads and stitches them with a twist into leather strips for a bracelet. In the fire pit across from her, the logs have burned down to hot coals. There's a pot of steaming coffee resting on a makeshift metal grill suspended atop legs of upended bricks above the coals. Thick slabs of peameal back bacon sizzle in a cast iron fry pan. A round of bannock is set off to one side. Ray emerges from the trailer pulling a dazzling white T-shirt over his head. He pours himself a mug of coffee and adds cream and sugar from small ceramic pots.

"Smells good." He pokes the bacon with a large fork and lazes his butt onto the edge of a rickety plastic chaise lounge. "They say we're in for a big dump of rain this afternoon." He

21

stares at the sky. There's not the faintest pale tendrils of anything that might be labelled a cloud formation. "Couldn't tell by looking now, eh?" He breaks off a chunk of bannock, swipes it through the bacon fat and takes a bite. "Mm, sweet." He spears a bacon slab, lays it on the bannock. "It's okay, yeah? There's enough?" He nods to Tantoo who ignores him and concentrates on her stitching. "Okay," he answers himself and bites in. "I mentioned I fixed the stove, right? You understand? The stove? Inside?" He points to the trailer and goes through various physical illustrations of what it means to be a stove or to resemble a stove. "The fuses were shot, is all. Each and every one of them. Inside the panel. Don't know how that would happen. That they'd all blow. Maybe it was like that when you moved in? Non-operational. I don't know. Maybe you got hit by lightning, huh? The camper? Do you remember? During a storm maybe? Lightning?" Again, he gestures with dramatic hand and arm movements, "*Lightning*? Flash! Zap! Ssssss ... No? Anyway, replaced them and that was it. Works like a hot damn! Even cleaned it. Gave it a good, old-fashioned scrub. The oven was a disaster. Practically had to chip at it with hammer and chisel. In fact, I scrubbed down the whole inside of the camper, top to bottom, in case you didn't notice. The shower stall was like a science project gone seriously bad. Put on a whole new showerhead. Adjustable spray. Nice. You know ... in case?"

He chews and swallows the remainder of the bannock and bacon.

"No need to thank me or anything. Just want to pull my weight. Beyond the rent, which is totally reasonable."

He squints at Tantoo. She raises her eyes to his and flashes a smile of gapped, chipped, and yellowed teeth. He doesn't know if she understands him or not. Whether she can talk or not, whether in English or Cree or anything, if at all. She uses pidgin sign language mostly. That and a list of very clear English prices scratched onto sticky notes when she's selling her merchandise. When a customer asks how much for a particular item she points, *this* for *that*. If they try to dicker for a lower price, she narrows her eyes quizzically and points again, *this* for *that*, like maybe they're a bit slow on the uptake and somehow missed the connection. They try again and she doesn't budge: *this* for *that* numb nuts, take it or leave it. They generally take it, figuring (probably) she's too thick to get through to. In all likelihood, she understands a hell of a lot more than she lets on, Ray guesses. She'd have to. Maybe she simply doesn't want to talk. And who can blame her? People treat her like shit as it is. If she didn't play the half-wit so convincingly well, they'd probably treat her worse. Probably lock her up in an institution somewhere. He licks his fingers clean of bacon fat.

Human fucking nature, he huffs.

"Anyway ..." He jumps to his feet and dusts his pant legs with a few hand slaps. "I'm heading into town and won't be back 'til late." He wags a finger at the fire. "No dinner for me, okay?" He points to his mouth and razors a line across his throat. The international sign, he thinks. Tantoo responds with a thumbnail dragged slowly, deliberately, across her skinny neck. She continues to grin like a maniac.

Shit, thinks Ray. It borders on the horrific.

"Good. You need anything?" He shakes his head up and down, back and forth. Tantoo waves three bony fingers that he takes as a no. Fine. He gives her a final look before he turns away. A strong wind would blow her like tumbleweed across the prairie, straight into the Hoodoos and she'd disappear without a trace, he thinks.

He hustles to his bike and clambers aboard. He has things to do, even if he isn't quite sure what, as yet.

ᕈ Weyburn—ninth-largest city in Saskatchewan, Canada. On the Souris River, 110 kilometres southeast of the provincial capital of Regina and 70 km north of the North Dakota border in the United States. The name is reputedly a corruption of the Scottish "wee burn," referring to a small creek. Population 11,000, give or take.

Ray cruises south on King Street. The landscape has definitely changed. Used to be flat as birdshit on the hood of a Buick, Ray's father was fond of saying in the good old days. If there ever was such a thing as 'the good old days,' time being a healer of all wounds and memory being less than a reliable source.

Nowadays, there are new buildings and businesses that have sprouted up everywhere: hotels, motels, restaurants, golf clubs, theatres, cultural centres. Even the ubiquitous urban sprawl with its mixed blight of blockbuster cinemas, fast-food chains, coffee shops, health food stores, banks, big box stores, gas stations, laundromats, along with the heavy stamp of identical, rowed, "little pink houses for you and me," as the popular song goes. Or went.

Ah, well, Ray thinks. People have to live somewhere. And I suppose if someone was feeling especially optimistic and/or generous—or even slightly hopeful—they could simply label it the natural progression of a town and be done with it. Hm.

He swings west on First Avenue then north into the

Souris Valley. He pulls up at an expanse of vacant acreage and shuts the bike's engine. Between a gridwork of paved streets, the property's divided into lot-sized sections using strung-together coloured wooden stakes. The lots have been flattened and cleared of the former premises and are prepped for the advance of heavy digging machinery. The site bears all the signs of a new housing sub-division about to be erected. The area in its entirety is surrounded by a tall metal fence capped with barbed wire and dotted with signs that read: NO TRESPASSING. KEEP OUT.

Friendly, Ray thinks.

At a distance further back, beyond the fence, Ray sees that the old woods are still standing. There were huts, he recollects, that were once an integral part of that same landscape and he wonders if they too remain, or if they were culled, razed and disposed of, along with the main building structures of the Asylum. Wouldn't surprise him, what with the connection the huts and the woods had with the inmates and the townsfolk at large.

Ah, the stories they could tell, Ray considers. Hell, those woods, and run-down huts were considered haunted back as long as I can remember, filled with unexplained sounds and shadows that scared the be-jeezus out of anyone brave or foolhardy or stupid enough to visit after dark. Evidence of troubled times and troubled minds and who needs that when you're trying to build a bright new future for people? Besides, it's not as if it was anything to be proud of. Best thing to do is just erase it, like an old stain. Unless, of course, it won't erase. A better idea? Why not build a freaking museum? Isn't that the usual fix? Cover the stain with a colourful Band-Aid. Fill the walls with photos of happy, smiling faces. People getting along. Folks playing musical instruments and dancing. Or hoisting hoes and shovels while working contentedly in the Asylum's gardens. Maybe add a small (very small) reference to the hangman's hut, citing hearsay and rumour so as to make it more of a myth than an actual fact. The outcome: an acceptable piece of money-making history.

"Paved Paradise, put up a parking lot." Another line from another popular song, though the Asylum wasn't much of a Paradise by all accounts.

Ray recalls his time exploring the woods and sneaking into the derelict building as a boy. Folks claimed the place was haunted by spirits of dead patients and even dead staff. Sure. Why wouldn't it be? It had a long dark history of deadly medical practices as well as being ravaged by Depression era dust storms and falling victim to the "White Plague": tuberculosis. Stories include a woman in heavy heels who paces the fourth floor late at night; a headless man who roams the halls cranking a coffee sifter; blank faces pressed against grimy windows; bodiless silhouettes that would brush against you. Scary stuff likely made even more unnerving by the fact it was a hospital for the insane. Prowling around those abandoned creepy corridors never failed to rattle Ray and whoever he was with, whether buddies, or his brother Ben, or sometimes a girlfriend out for a cheap thrill—a chance to steal a kiss or cop a feel beneath the full moon—all the while waiting for the ghosts to appear or the axe to fall. Otherwise, as a false show of bravado, Ray would piss in a corner or take a dump on the floor, even bust a window or two—of what few windows remained—like every other kid who dared enter. Though, more often than not, he'd end by flying out the door, into the night, having heard a scream or a moan or a cry of what he took to be some poor trapped soul being dunked in ice water or given a shot of electricity to the brain.

Ray lets out a low laugh and shakes his head. He leans on his bike with his arms folded and surveys the scene. It doesn't look like anything to be frightened of now, he tells himself, in its present state: flat and empty. Just the same, he thinks, there are some things you can't destroy by simply knocking down or building over. Some things you can't cover with rows of houses and sets of new drapes and fresh coats of paint. Some things you can't kill no matter what you do or how hard you try. In the end, some things are either too deeply ingrained or too stubborn to just give up and go off quietly to die. Too bad, so sad. He takes a last cursory look, cranks the engine, puts the bike in gear and pulls away.

~ Ray saunters into the Detour Bar and Grill. It seems busy for a weekday afternoon. Though, maybe not, given it's Happy Hour and half-price on the food menu. That's a draw. Men are perched at the rail drinking beer and watching the various sports on the various TVs that occupy every corner. People sit at tables talking with each other over drinks, finger food and fries. There's a group of guys and gals shooting pool. Ray recognizes several of them and marches over. They perform the ritual shoulder slaps and high fives, ask whassup? What's happening? And so on.

"Who needs a beer?" Ray asks. "My shout." He calls for the waitress to bring a pitcher and another glass.

The gang shoots the shit a while. Someone tells Ray to grab a stick and join in on a game. Loser pays for the table.

He says no, but maybe he'll take their money later if they were that eager to part with it. Everyone laughs: *yeah, right, as if,* and so on. Everyone friendly, laid back, here for a good time. Ray waves a hand in the air for another pitcher; after more small talk he takes his beer glass to an empty table by the window and settles in to peruse a menu. He looks up just as he feels a shadow fall over him. Two men loom, similar in age to him. One is hefty, wearing a Roughriders ball cap. The other's built like a lumpy Sumo wrestler; his beer gut hangs out below his soiled and faded AC/DC Black Ice World Tour T-shirt. There's a sudden rumble of rolling thunder followed by a crash of rain outside the window. The street alternates from dark to light and dark again as thick clouds race past overhead, alive with pockets of furious lightning bolts.

Coincidence or omen, Ray wonders.

"Hey, Ray."

"Hey, yourself."

"Remember me?"

Ray flashes a wide smile and shrugs. "Should I?"

The guy with the ball cap does all the talking. What little there is.

"Barry Leask."

The man's cursed with a thick Neanderthal forehead and a unibrow that often identifies a person as just south of moronic. Sometimes mistakenly, though in this particular instance, there's some evidence of truth.

"Oh, yeah, Barry. Long time no see. How're things?"

"You know."

"Sure, sure. Still playin' the old six-string?" Ray mimes a riff on air guitar. It's from The Beatles tune, "Day Tripper."

"Brrrrr-roww-rowwwww-rowwwww ..." His hand slides up and down the neck.

"I never played guitar," Barry deadpans.

"Oh, yeah, that's right. Too bad, I was thinkin' about startin' a band."

"That a fact."

"Thinkin' about it, yeah. Givin' it some serious consideration. Callin' it The One-eyed Trouser Snakes."

"Oh, yeah?"

"Yeah. Whaddya think?"

"I think you're fulla shit."

"You might be right. *May be.* Sure. 'Course, either way, I still need to find me a *gi*-tar player. Who's your quiet friend?"

Ray figures him for Japanese. Or at least partially. Both men have a veneer of dry white dust and plaster embedded in their brows, under their eyes, on their arms and spattered into their clothing, likely from construction work. Drywall or concrete? He isn't sure. Evidence of primer paint as well. A stubborn mix of materials you basically have to scrape off using steaming hot water and an SOS pad, more often than not, taking a layer of skin along with it.

"This here's Ki."

Ray considers saying *hi, Ki,* or *yippee-ki-yi,* then doesn't. Why push it? Besides, it's too easy. "Nice to meet you."

"No, it ain't." Barry straightens and puts his hands on his hips. Ki folds his arms across his barrel chest.

"Okay, have it your way." Ray rests on his elbows, his beer glass turning between his fingertips. "Somethin' on your tiny pea-pickin' brain, Barry?"

"Why you here? I mean, really."

"Here?" Ray looks around the bar.

"In town, I mean. What's your game? Why're you back?"

"Oh, you know, visiting family. Getting re-acquainted with old friends, such as yourself. Taking in the sights."

"Bullshit."

"You asked. I'm telling."

"I'm gonna say this once. Stay away from my sister."

"You're joking, right? Now, what would I possibly want with your sister?" Ray grins ear to ear and speaks in a *nudge-nudge-wink-wink* tone of voice. "I mean, that I didn't already have years ago?"

Barry flinches. "Don't fuck with me."

"Tell me something, Barry. Are you actually as ignorant or stupid as you look and sound, or is it some kind of act for my benefit?"

"We have some unfinished business, asshole."

"Yeah, I was gonna say, a good dentist can perform miracles these days, huh? You look good. Can hardly tell they were missing." Ray taps his front teeth with a fingernail tip.

"You blindsided me, bastard. If I'd known you were gonna take a swing, it would've been a different story."

"Yeah, and if my aunt had balls, she'd be my uncle."

"You think you're funny? I got back-up now."

"You mean the Hai Karate kid, here? Shit, I've jumped over bigger than him in a fight just to get to the men."

Barry makes two fists, grinds his knuckles into the tabletop and leans his face close to Ray's.

"You laugh now, pal, but I'm telling you, we're not done. I owe you."

"Yeah, we are done, Barry. Now, why don't you take your goon and bugger off before I do something you'll regret?"

"Keep talking smart ass. It's just a matter of time."

"What's just a matter of time?" Ben joins the action. His shoulders are soaked, and he shakes rainwater from his hat. Barry stands tall and flexes his hands. "Anything I can do to help?"

"Hey, Ben. Nice to see ya. The fellas came over to welcome me back to town. Pretty nice of them, don't ya think?"

"Being neighbourly, is that it?" Ben asks, and the two men nod.

"They even invited me to play in their rock and roll band —what was the name again?" Ray snaps his fingers. There's no response. "Ah, well, doesn't matter. Barry-boy still has to learn to master the old six-string, anyway. Right, Barry?"

More air guitar from Ray.

"Yeah, that's right." Barry chews on his lower lip. "We'll be seein' you around, Ray. Ben. S'long."

"You boys don't wanna stay and chat a little longer? Maybe join me for a friendly beer?"

"No, we gotta get a move on. Things to do. Another time, though. Count on it."

"I'll look forward to it. We'll do lunch maybe. Or I'll drop over for dinner. Maybe meet the wife and kids."

"Yeah, maybe," Barry snorts.

"Hey, Barry! High school joke. Maybe you'll appreciate it. It's been raining cats and dogs all day. Two students standing outside their lockers hanging up their soggy jackets. Boy asks girl, did you get your hair wet this morning? Girl says, why no, I didn't. Boy says, really? What'd you do, pee through a straw?" Ray gives a horse laugh and smacks the tabletop with his palms.

Barry doesn't know what to say. His mouth hangs open, like, *what the fuck?*

"Later," he says, and points a finger. Ki leads him out of the bar by the arm.

Ben takes a seat as the pair exits. He hangs his hat on his knee. The storm's already easing and the sound of thunder fades into the distance.

"What was that?"

"Apparently Barry's the type that holds a grudge."

"Long memory and short fuse. Bad combination. You'll be wise to watch your back."

"That's kind of what he said. I figure he's mostly blowing smoke out his ass. Clowns to the left of me, jokers to the right. All talk, yeah?"

"Maybe, maybe not. He was trouble for a while. He's settled down over the years. Married with kids and a steady job'll do that. Plus, he's put on a few extra pounds. Still, he's started working out in the gym, I hear. Racquetball, weights. You wanna be careful, just in case."

"Will do. Anyway, you weren't just in the neighbourhood, I'm guessing."

"You're right. I came looking for you."

"How'd you know I'd be here?"

"Small town. There's no hiding. Besides, I understand you've been tossing money around here at the Detour—and elsewhere—lately, like there's no tomorrow. Buying drinks for the house and so on."

"Not as bad as that, though I'm sure there's some folks believing I'm Gatsby returned from the tropics with my pockets lined with thousand-dollar bills."

"And you're not?"

"Far from it, little brother. Story gets bigger the more it's told, that's all."

"Then what's the deal?"

"Just trying to score a few points among the locals. Ease a few minds. Soothe a few wounds. Open a few doors. Have a little fun."

"Uh-huh. I did some checking up on you. I hope you don't mind."

"Comes with the job, right? Find anything useful or interesting I should know about?" Ray sips his beer. "You want?" he asks, and Ben motions, no.

"I got diddly-squat. There's nothing. Nada. It's like you never existed. How is that, Ray? How do you go out and live in the world for years and leave no trace? No indication of a place of residence, no record of a job, no income tax filed ... Driver's license and insurance still lists our old house address where we grew up. According to all sources, you never left Weyburn. You're like a ghost. How'd you survive Ray?"

"C'mon, Ben ... You know there's always a lonesome generous soul out there willing to take in a stray. Provide a roof and a meal and so on."

"You mean a woman."

"Generally speaking."

"What about money? They give you that too?"

"Why, Ben, you're not trying to make me feel guilty, are you?" Ray grins broadly and laughs. "If they gave me money, believe me, I earned it for services rendered. At least, no one ever complained. Except when I left. Then it was all tears and histrionics. Boo-hoo, boo-hoo."

"Uh-huh."

"Otherwise, there's a whole underground workforce out there, which I'm sure you're aware of, it's no secret. I picked fruit, repaired machinery, dug holes, did plumbing, did electrics, hung drywall, painted walls ..."

"That's quite the skill set you developed."

"Not so tough. Keep my eyes and ears open, ask a few detailed questions, sound interested, don't be afraid to make mistakes. So long as nobody dies, right? Check out a YouTube video if I'm really stuck. Generally, it's the same steps for everything—insert tab A into slot B. Flip a switch when necessary. Doesn't take a genius. You could train a monkey. Do the job, get paid cash money on the barrelhead, move on, no papers to fill out, nothing to sign, no embarrassing questions to answer. Screw the man, baby."

"Uh-huh. What about the bike?"

"The bike?"

"Triumph Thunderbird 900 Classic. Circa 1995 or so, I'm guessing. Excellent shape. Must've cost you some serious coin."

The waitress approaches. "Anything on the menu strike your fancy?"

"Wings," says Ray. "Spicy, with fries."

"Sure. Another beer?"

"Sure." Ray hands her his empty glass and rocks his head. "That's a funny story, about the bike."

"I like funny stories."

"Ben, you say that, but you're so fucking ..." Ray makes a dour, strained face. "Sombre. Like you're constipated and haven't had a good shit in days." He grunts and chuckles. Ben doesn't budge. "Same old Ben. So, okay. I was working a few months for some guy who owned a scrap metal yard. Automobile graveyard and whatever. We'd crush big odd-shaped shit into little square-shaped shit and send it off to become some other kind of consumable shit. The ultimate recyclers. Other guys working there talked about how their cars were put together from parts of other cars and no big deal. Help yourself. So, one day I found the twisted frame and engine of the Triumph and went about picking through the garbage for bent and rusted bits and pieces I could fix up so as to reassemble the machine in more or less original pristine condition."

A beer arrives. "Here ya go, honey," the waitress says.

Ray takes a healthy swig through the foam and burps, *pardon me*. He wipes his upper lip with the back of a finger.

"Anyway, got the bastard painted up, buffed and polished so it shone like a new dime. Engine purred like a goddamn kitten. Meanwhile, Hugo—the owner of the scrap yard—gets wind of what I'm doing and sniffs out where I've got the bike stored. He's obviously impressed. One look and he decides I should pay him for it since I ..." Ray uses his fingers as quotes, "... 'stole' the parts from his property. I decided it wouldn't do me any good to say the other guys did the same thing. It was easy enough to tell, he wasn't in a mood to listen. He had his own agenda. I'd obviously done too good a job on the repair, and he wanted a cut. A big cut. I told him I was willing to pay him the scrap price for the materials I scavenged. He turned me down flat and told me he wanted such-and-such ridiculous amount of money or else he'd take the bike, and if I argued, he'd call the cops and charge me with theft over."

The finger food arrives. Ray grabs a fry and twirls it in a paper container of ketchup. He tosses the fry into his mouth and chews.

"Nice guy, huh?"

"Yeah. What'd you do?"

"This is the funny part. I know he's too fucking lazy to walk, so he parks his car in the rear of the office shed, right smack in the demolition area. Everyone's supposed to know and keep hands off, right? Right. The next afternoon, when he comes looking for me to seal the deal, he finds me there, at the controls in the cab of the loading crane. I say, look up, and there's his expensive Jag convertible hanging in a chain harness sixty feet above the ground. Well, he turns white as a freaking sheet and his jaw drops. I figure he's wet himself or worse. I'll call the cops, he says. I tell him: Go ahead. How was I to know it was your car? I'm not paid to think. Not my fault it was parked in the wrong place, among the other wrecks. Besides, I'm not even a real employee here. As far as you and the account books are concerned, I don't exist." Ray clicks his tongue and grins. "Well, that shut him up pretty quick. I tell him he has a choice, either sign the bike over to me as used parts for fifty bucks, or else I accidentally flip the switch and his vehicle's trash." Ray shrugs like it's a *fait accompli*. "I hand him a slip of paper and he scribbles his name on the dotted line. I jump out, drop a bright orange fifty on the seat and leave him to save his Jag. Next, I snatch the bike and burn rubber out of the lot. Kiss my bony ass, sweetheart."

"You still have the paper?"

"Are you kidding? Yeah. You wanna see it?"

"No need. Just want to make sure." Ben sits solid as Buddha.

"Something else?" Ray pushes the fries toward Ben who drags a few into his mouth and grinds methodically. He swallows.

"Last question, I promise. Then we move on. Relax. Enjoy each other's company. Okay? Be a family again."

"Shit, Ben ... You're scarin' me."

"Why'd you come back, Ray? What do you want? What are you after?"

"Funny. That's what Barry asked."

"It's the million-dollar question, Ray. It's what's on everyone's mind."

"Sonofabitch. Why is that, I wonder?"

"Natural human curiosity, I suppose."

"There's nothing natural about human curiosity, Ben. We both know that. There's always something else going on below the surface. Something not quite right."

"Such as?"

"I don't know. Beth mentioned fear."

"You didn't exactly leave town on a positive note, Ray. In fact, you'd managed to piss off any number of people, one way or another over the years. You can hardly blame them for wondering *what-the-hell*?"

"They've been watching too many bad movies. They're worried I'm going to murder them in their beds."

Ben smiles a crooked smile and crinkles his brow. "So? Maybe you owe it to everyone. Some kind of explanation. Give the people a reason to take a calm breath and go about their own business. Why come back? Why now? What do want, Ray? What are you after?"

"I'll be honest with you, Ben. I don't owe any of these cocksuckers anything. Whatever they think about me, whatever happened or whatever they think happened, that's their concern and I don't give a rat's ass." Ray takes a slow breath and drinks from his glass. "But for you and for Beth ..." He squints across the table and the features of his face sag, and his voice goes soft. He almost speaks, then applies the brakes. "Promise you won't laugh, 'cause ..."

"I won't laugh, Ray."

"Okay. I've been having dreams, Ben. Strange dreams. Bad dreams. Nightmares, I guess you'd say. And I don't know where they come from or what they mean, but they have something to do with this place, and I aim to find out what."

Ben reaches over, grabs hold of Ray's beer glass, raises it to his mouth and takes two deep swallows. He puts the glass down and drums the tabletop with his fingers. "That's quite the thing," he says.

"Yeah," Ray says nodding. "Yeah. It's something all right."

"I don't quite know what to say or how to respond to that."

"I hear ya."

The two stare at each other and laugh. Ben covers a cough with a hand.

"Is part of your search to go and visit dad?"

"It's on my *to-do* list."

"He's moved. Just outside McTaggart. Couldn't live in the house anymore. Said there were too many memories in the walls. Locked the door and walked away. Says we can sell it when he's gone. Not that it's worth much, it isn't. Lives like a hermit in a run-down shack on a piece of dirt. Resembles a skeleton with eyes."

"I've been told."

"Makes his own wine and beer. Grows his own tobacco. Eats all his food out of tin cans and glass jars. Or sealed bags. Says it's the only way he can be sure it's safe."

"You think he's gone senile or something?"

"The doctors say no. That's when we managed to get him in for tests, which is a while back. He fought tooth and nail. 'Course, with the doctors, he was on his best behaviour. Sweet and gentle as a lamb. Did everything they asked. No muss, no fuss. Polite, jokey, friendly. Probably picked up a few tricks from his days working in the mental ward. Anyway, they couldn't determine anything considered critically wrong. Nothing they could pinpoint and put a name to, y'know? Nothing clinical. Though, it's obvious to anyone, he's definitely suffering some certain degree of paranoia."

"Hell, Ben, we're all of us suffering some certain degree of paranoia. Otherwise, we wouldn't be human. I'm asking is he losing his mind?"

"When you see him, you decide. I take a drive out there on occasion to check how he's doing. Beth won't allow the kids anymore. Can't blame her. They get upset." Ben smacks his hat on his thigh, squeezes water from the brim, and sets it on the table.

Ray wags a finger. "It's bad luck to put a hat on the table," he says.

"Oh, yeah? And why's that?"

"Some believe it brings a quarrel into the house by the end of the day. Others believe it's because hats can spread lice. Still others are of the opinion that evil spirits live in the hair."

"Uh-huh. So, nothing good in any case." Ben removes the hat from the table and drops it on the chair beside him.

"Now someone's gonna get a wet ass from a chair seat." Ray laughs.

"Like I said, nothing good." Ben laughs along. "Anyway,

you wanna share with me the nature of those dreams you're having? Maybe I can shed some light. Maybe not. I'm no psychiatrist, but it might help to talk it out. What do you think?"

"Yeah, okay. Why not?" Ray dumps hot sauce on the wings and tears into the flesh. "Mm," he says. "Tasty. Go on, try them. I just need a minute to think where to begin if that's okay. So, it doesn't sound more *unreal* or crazy than it already is."

"Sure, Ray. Take your time."

Ben leans in on an elbow, resting his chin on the knuckles of one hand. He tries to imagine what these dreams might entail; what they could contain that has Ray so spooked. Family life wasn't all roses growing up, sure, but theirs wasn't much different from every other family's situation around them, and you learned to take the good with the bad. Nothing out of the ordinary so far as he could recall. Unless it's something to do with their mother? Something still unresolved. Something still eating at Ray. Ben takes a deep breath and blows air out through his nose. He's at a loss. Nothing to do except wait and allow Ray to tell his story. Which he does, in his own time.

4.

*"But are not all facts dreams as soon
as we put them behind us?"*

—Emily Dickinson, *The Gorgeous Nothings*

t's evening. The sky is unblemished except for the hovering moon and bright spill of the Milky Way. Up ahead, a fire roars behind the camper trailer. Sparks rise in waves from the blaze, flicker for a time, then disappear into the blackness. Ray can spot the scene clearly as he tears around a slight bend in the road. Drawing nearer, he sees the familiar bent shape of Tantoo circling the flames, her lithe body slowly dipping and weaving. A pipe dangles from her lips. He recognizes the spectacle as one of her numerous ritual prayer ceremonies. Whether in homage to the moon spirit or the Trickster god or to the coyotes who yip and yowl from the tops of low hills, Ray isn't sure. He doesn't even know if Tantoo is sure. Whatever it is, when the mood or the impulse strikes, she seems compelled to perform some kind of fire dance aimed to honour or appease something or someone. Her arms stretch above her head and her hands and fingers twist into a myriad of shapes, and Ray wonders if this might be a form of sign language, she uses to convey a message or tell a story. Not that it means anything to Ray one way or another since it's a language he finds impossible to decipher. Still, he can't help but be curious.

He can smell the burning wood. As well, sweetgrass smolders in bowls adding its own distinct vanilla aroma to the smoky surroundings.

Ray wheels into the yard, turns off the engine, stands the bike, goes over, and follows Tantoo's path around the fire, allowing a comfortable distance between them so as not to interfere with her movements or break her concentration. He's taken to studying her performances closely in an attempt to discover some sort of identifiable pattern that might allow him access to the specific ritual. As usual, all her dance movements and hand gestures appear random or improvised, like previous episodes, but never the same. Tantoo suddenly freezes, stopping Ray in his tracks. He feels it's unlikely that he was seen, and that Tantoo has an uncanny ability to sense his presence. She turns, and with a dramatic sweeping arm motion, presents him with the pipe. He takes it by the bowl, sticks the mouthpiece between his lips, and sucks the smoke into his lungs. He rears back his head, beats his chest with a fist, and lets out an animal howl. Tantoo bounces on her heels, grins, and claps her hands gleefully. Ray takes another deep puff. So far, he's been able to determine the bowl contains a mixture of store-bought Mexican *salvia divinorum* and a type of locoweed that Tantoo cultivates in her own garden for 'medicinal' purposes and spiritual healing. All perfectly legal, though there are rumblings within the judiciary and the public at large to either control or else ban the exotic herb altogether. In their correct proportion, the dried plants provide the partaker with a general feeling of euphoria, as well as being capable of evoking visions that can best be described as otherworldly, even mystical, much the same as Carlos Castañeda's use of peyote to explore Toltec shamanism. Ray recalls the book he'd read—*The Teachings of Don Juan: A Yaqui Way of Knowledge*—that dealt with exploring connections between such shrubs or weeds and the interpretation of dreams.

Most often perceived by governing bodies as illicit, these commonly available and naturally growing flora have always been a quick means to achieving an altered state of consciousness. The desired upshot being to increase awareness and expand powers of perception. In short, a mild hallucinogen. Get the proportions wrong, however, and it can spell a recipe for disaster, leading to a "bad" trip: experiencing disturbing images; having feelings of extreme anxiety or terror; having feelings of deep, dark despair; having the sensation of bugs crawling along the skin, and so on. In other words, all hell can break loose, and you can end up with a nasty case of fried brain cells.

Ray's still a newbie, so he feels the effects of the smoky mixture almost immediately. Everything turns to slow motion and his eyelids grow heavy, making them difficult to keep open. His knees turn to mush and buckle under his weight. As he slumps slowly to the ground, Tantoo expertly relieves him of the pipe. Her face fills with silent laughter.

That's it for you, Gringo! She seems to say. *Enjoy the ride.*

Ray stretches out on the buffalo grass and gazes skyward. Orion's belt, he murmurs. Wesakaychak in Cree. Hunter. Trickster. He tries to focus but finds it increasingly difficult. He doesn't know if he's viewing the stars through open eyes or if the stars are burning pinholes through his closed eyelids or if he only imagines he sees stars. Then again, what does it matter? A man dreams he's a butterfly dreaming he's a man or *vice versa* ... Who's to know where the dream ends, and reality begins? Or if there is a reality. Maybe we only dream we exist. Who's to judge? God? And who judges God? Me, evidently, answers Crow, choking a jagged fishbone down its black-feathered throat.

What the fuck?! Ray's mind obviously adrift and spinning rapidly into the ether. Where does all this come from? he wonders. These ideas. These images. Constellation names. A fragment of Chinese philosophy courtesy of Zhuangzi. A line of poetry from Ted Hughes. Random, or what? Who knows? Who cares? Whether asleep or awake or asleep and dreaming he's awake, what's the difference? His body feels nailed to the ground and his mind's been hijacked. He has no choice except to give over and let whatever happens, happen.

He pictures himself under a blazing sun running naked through a field of sweetgrass. Nothing new in this. In most of his recent dreams he's naked or gets naked, rips the clothes from his body and flings them into the air. He has no idea why he runs or where he's running to. His single aim is to run. His pace is steady, rhythmical, his breath deep and even, his ochre-coloured skin shows a healthy glow beneath a thin layer of sweat. He weaves comfortably among the tall fragrant grass, sometimes leaping to clear a mound of rubble or avoid a rut or prairie dog hole. Upon reaching the bank of a dried-out gully, the soil gives way, he loses his footing and tumbles to the bottom of the stony bed where he bangs his forehead on a sharp rock. He rolls onto his back and uses his elbows to push himself into a sitting position. There's a nasty gash below the hairline. A thread of blood oozes across his eyebrow and down his cheek. He swipes at the blood with his fingertips and rubs it with a thumb, as if to convince himself it's his. Suddenly, a shadow envelops him. He tips his chin. His gaze is met by a dark blurred figure haloed in intense sunlight, what he takes to be a man standing over him. He's a bit woozy from the blow to the head and blinks a number of times in an attempt to gain a clearer picture. He rubs his eyes with the backs of his hands, shakes his head, squints. The aura surrounding the figure, the man, is blinding, almost painfully so. He lowers his vision to the feet, where he's able to zero in, then slowly climb his eyes upward. The man wears laced brown shoes, khaki leggings with matching baggy-kneed knickers, a brown belt, a button-down collared khaki shirt decorated with various badges and insignia on the pockets and a large red neckerchief knotted at the throat. The light again becomes unbearable and Ray cups his hands around his eyes to shade them from the glare. He strains to try to discover a face attached to the uniformed body. Instead, he sees that the man wears a brown paper bag over his head and is saluting him with two stiff fingers placed smartly at the bag's folded edge.

Ray wakes in a sweat, his breath choppy. He's lying outside the camper trailer on the ground, still clothed so far as he can tell. The fire's gone cold and he's covered in a thick blanket. The sun's in the east and rising he reckons, so he hasn't missed morning. He sits up and touches his forehead. Nothing. No blood, no cut. He does a quick recap of his dream. He's familiar with some of the images. He's dreamt them before, though in different or varying combinations. He's even done research.

Being naked is easy, he recalls from his reading: You're seen for who you are. The dry riverbed? A sign of loss: You've run out of options or hit a rut in your life. No shit, Sherlock!

The image of a cut forehead often symbolizes a loss of authority and a sense of humiliation. Great, just what I need. Another popular interpretation is that some sort of hidden treasure will be revealed, although at a price—go figure—and there's always a danger the prize will be lost, naturally. There is, as well, the accompanying fear and apprehension of said loss to be suffered. Ain't it swell, he laughs! So far, so good. Nothing out of the ordinary, except: What the fuck is it about a saluting boy scout with a paper bag over his head? That's a first. And it might even stump Freud. Be prepared, isn't that the motto? For what and why? Who knows? Anyway, Ben was the model boy scout, not me.

Tantoo approaches. She offers him a hot cup of coffee. He tosses the blanket, sits up and takes the brew. He blows on it and sucks in a mouthful of liquid. It's sweet and creamy, just the way he likes it. Tantoo doesn't miss much, he thinks. She squats across from him, wraps her arms around her knees, and flashes a smile.

"You used the stove, yes?" Ray says. "Good for you. The stove"—he mimes the preparation. "To make the coffee."

Tantoo tosses her head and shuts her eyes. Ray wonders if she maybe understands him. If maybe he's communicating to her on some basic level. If maybe she's proud of herself. Of her accomplishment. She lets out a satisfied sigh. That's when he realizes—it's got nothing to do with him or the stove or communicating—she's taking a relaxed piss on the ground.

Fine, thinks Ray, and laughs. Just fine. It's good to be around someone who has their priorities straight.

He watches the urine steadily flow from beneath Tantoo's skirts; watches as it percolates and carves a small bubbly tributary in the dry red dust; watches as it abruptly halts and soaks into the landscape, leaving nothing but a damp scar.

～ Beth's working an extra shift at the diner over the lunch hour. One of the staff called in sick. Often, it's the summer help. Young and restless. Likely the twenty-six-ounce flu or too much sun from hanging out at the beach the day before. Or they're just plain bored. She's happy to oblige. There's always a neighbour available to watch the kids and she likes spending a few hours outside of the house to be with adults. She enjoys the work; enjoys the idea of wearing an apron, of having a receipt book tucked in the front pouch and a pencil stuck under her hair behind an ear; enjoys handing out menus; enjoys chatting with staff and customers, asking, 'What'll it be?' or 'More coffee?' or 'How's your day going?' It's like being paid to meet up with friends, she tells everyone. Except today, where a cataclysmic change has occurred. All anyone wants to talk to her about is Ray. Ray this. Ray that. What the fuck? They won't come right out and ask the burning question, no. They beat around the bush. They ask: How is he? What's he like? Has he changed? Is it true that he ...? I remember when he ... Fill in the blank.

Everyone has a story about Ray or to do with Ray as to why he left town and what he's been doing since. 'I heard that' ... someone would say, or 'I was told that'..., or 'I'm sure I read somewhere that' ... and so on and so forth. A string of speculation from marriage to mayhem to murder. None of it true, as far as Beth is aware, and she conveys as much to them in short simple phrases, polite but firm. Naturally, they don't believe her, confronting her frequently with the supposed trump card of her being *kin,* even *ex-girlfriend,* and so she should have the inside scoop. The conversations continue in this fashion throughout her shift and Beth begins to feel more than slightly put on the spot, if not outright attacked, as she gets the distinct impression that folks are becoming excessively angered and irritated with her perceived evasiveness. What begins as idle curiosity soon ramps to impassioned pleas. 'Surely to God, Beth!' they argue. 'You must know something? He must have told you something. Why won't you share it with us? We're your friends and neighbours. Tell us, for *chrissakes*, please! Throw us a bone, we're begging you.'

Begging? she thinks. Wow!

What she'd like to do is tell them to get a grip people and relax. She's as much in the dark as they are, and what does it matter? Instead, she excuses herself to see to another table. Not that it makes much difference. When the diner patrons don't speak directly to her, they converse and whisper amongst themselves. What do they gossip about? Doesn't take a rocket scientist to figure that one out, Beth shrugs. Ray, of course. Who and what else? The phrase 'disruptive influence' suddenly enters Beth's mind. She cleans tables and plunks down fresh plates and silverware as she considers the word 'disruptive' more closely: characterized by unrest, disorder and/or insubordination. Unruly, rowdy, rebellious. She grunts a quiet laugh, *ha*, grabs a full coffee pot and circles the room, topping up empty or half-empty mugs, dropping cream and sugar packets as she goes. She considers the word 'influence': the capacity to have an effect on the character, development or behaviour of someone or something. Holy shit! she thinks. That fits Ray to a freaking

'T' all right. He's barely arrived back in town and already he's got everyone buzzing. She can't help but be somewhat impressed by the reaction and wonders: What had anyone in this place talked about before today? What had anyone talked about in this place *ever* before Ray resurfaced in all his mystery? Before Ray re-entered their quiet and boring lives? The answer? Nothing. She stands behind the counter and surveys the scene. She rocks her head back and forth and pops her lips. The thought of providing some of her own style of mischief enters her mind—let's give 'em somethin' to talk about—she sings under her breath. Tell them Ray's returned home 'cause he's suffering stage four pancreatic cancer or dying of AIDS or has an inoperable brain tumour or whatnot. Something tragically romantic. An ailment taken straight out of a cheap paperback novel or tear-jerker Hollywood film. It might be fun, though, maybe not. She has the sneaking suspicion that no one in this crowd would get her dark sense of humour and wouldn't understand that it's meant as a joke. In fact, it's the sort of news they probably expect to hear, maybe even hope for, so she decides not to go there. They'll only be disappointed when the story turns out to be false, and then, they'll take it out on her, for sure.

This strained behaviour between Beth and the customers continues on in the same or similar fashion until mid-afternoon. Even the other staff members gaze at her oddly—the fry cook in back who's never interested in anyone or anything beyond what's written on the order slip and served on the plate peers out with curious eyes and leans an ear against the small round window of the kitchen's swinging door to catch some indication of Beth as she possibly drops a word or a clue. Maybe they're right. Maybe she should know what's really going on with Ray, but she doesn't. What she does know is that Ray has managed to ruin her day while not even being physically present, while not even being remotely aware.

What am I? she thinks. Chopped liver? Christ! If you're all so eager to know anything, why not track him down and ask him yourselves?! Bunch of simpering cowards, she mumbles, discarding her apron, walking furiously out the door, onto the sidewalk and up the street, her shift over.

～ Ben wasn't exaggerating. The place is a run-down shack complete with collapsing wood frame, busted and decayed board siding, broken windowpanes stuffed with burlap sacking or wads of newsprint and a weather-beaten shingled roof that threatens to cave. Dilapidated outhouse at the side, storage hut with the door hanging by a single bent hinge, water pump with a cracked blue plastic bucket under the spout, empty propane tanks scattered about, along with shattered bits of furniture and rusty machine and bicycle parts. Remnants of a wood fence off to one side of the shack, the few pickets that remain attached are split and rotted, while the majority have long since fallen and lie derelict on the ground.

Ray eases the bike around back. Some distance across the dirt lot, a lone man sits in a folding canvas beach chair baking in the mid-day sun. Heat rises from the parched ground in waves giving the scene a surreal feel to it. The man turns his head slightly, alerted by the rumble of the bike engine. He sports a sweat-yellowed Edmonton Eskimo ball cap and a pair of dollar store sunglasses. He sips wine from a red plastic juice glass. Ray settles the bike and ambles toward the man. He stands beside him and stares out over the empty prairie.

"Flat as birdshit on the hood of a Buick," Ray comments.

"Got that right." The man coughs up a wad of phlegm and spits. He appears otherwise unperturbed by the interruption.

"How ya doin' stranger? Remember me?"

"Ha! The prodigal son returns." The man bolds the statement with a sweep of a hooked hand in the air, as if he's framing a movie title. "To what do I owe the pleasure of your visit?"

"I was in the neighbourhood. Thought I'd stop by and say hello. Chew the fat, shoot the breeze. You know, catch up on old times."

"You haven't changed a bit, Ray. You're as full of shit now as you ever were. Also, the same smug, self-satisfied brand of humour." He leans his body opposite, drops his shoulders over the chair arm and pops the lid on a blue and white Coleman cooler, affixed with wheels and a handle for easy transport. "I got wine and I got beer. Don't expect a label. Make it myself. Name your poison."

"A beer."

"Sorry, no glass." He opens the beer cap with his teeth, passes the bottle to Ray and flicks the metal cap onto a growing pile. "No chair either. I wasn't expecting company."

"Bottle's good. I see you still don't own an opener." Ray drags the cooler a couple of feet to the side and plunks himself down on the lid. The two men drink and ponder. "You've got ice. How do you manage that?"

"Comes in bags. Pure glacial water. I have it delivered. Keep it in the freezer. Got the number on my cell, speed dial."

"You own a cell?"

"Doesn't everyone?"

"Yeah, apparently."

"You thought I was maybe too ... what?"

"Nothing. I was just surprised, that's all. That you needed one, given ..." Ray gives a half-ass look around.

"Uh-huh."

There's an uncomfortable silence between the two as they stare blankly into the distance. They're both well aware that this conversation is heading nowhere, except down the toilet. Neither was ever much for small talk. Or any talk, for that matter. Ray's dad swishes wine in his mouth, swallows, then grits his teeth. Someone has to say something, he thinks, and it might as well be him.

"What do you want, Ray?"

"Okay, yeah. Down to it. Came to ask you a few questions."

"About what?"

"Mom, mainly."

"Bit late for that, isn't it? She's dead and gone for some time."

"Yeah, I was thinking more, well, before that. I was seven when it happened. I don't really remember much about her. I don't know what she was like. I don't know who she was or how the two of you met or anything, really. It's a blank."

"Why shouldn't it be? It was none of your goddamn business then and it's even less so now." He clears his throat and sucks air through his stained teeth.

"Is that a fact?"

"C'mon, Ray. Since when did you go getting all nostalgic and sentimental?"

"All you ever told me and Ben was that she was a troubled woman. You wouldn't say anything more about it. What did you mean by that?"

"You sure you want to open that box of hurt?"

"I think so, yeah. It's been eating at me for a few years, and it won't go away. I need to know."

"Uh-huh." The man takes a healthy swig from his glass. "I get it. Something's going on. What is it?"

He points a crooked index finger at Ray. The nail's grown long, thick, and grey. Also curved, like a talon. It's the same with the rest of his fingernails.

"You're worried you're going to turn out like her, is that it? Afraid your mind might snap? Afraid you might do some harm to yourself? And you think it might be hereditary? Don't make me laugh. Let me tell you something, Ray-boy. Your mother had reasons for what went wrong with her. Hard, strong, actual reasons. She had a tough go of it growing up. Things she never got over. Led to psychological problems off and on. She had a genuine condition. You? You got nothing. You sprang out of the womb damaged goods. You always had a chip on your shoulder. You always had a cocky attitude that you were somehow superior to everyone else, and the world owed you something. You never cared about anyone or anything other than yourself. If you're fucked in the head, you brought it on yourself, okay? Ask me how or why? I don't know. Look at Ben. The pair of you are like night and day. Total opposites. How does that happen, huh? Both raised the same way. It's a goddamn puzzle is what it is. A puzzle that leaves me scratching my head. There's nothing that jumps out; nothing I can put my finger on. What I do know for sure though is, beyond the shadow of a doubt, the fault's in you, not your mother. You need someone to blame, look in a mirror."

Ray sits still and attentive, leaning in, allowing his dad's harsh words to wash over him. He doesn't argue, doesn't lash back. When he figures his dad's tirade is over and done, Ray straightens and rolls his shoulders.

"Maybe that's true," he says, calmly. "I'd still like to know, though. What reasons? What happened? Why all the secrecy? The silence. I mean, according to stories I heard, *your* mother died under suspicious circumstances, yeah? Weren't you ever curious?"

"*My* mother? Why you bringing her into this? It was sudden. I was told it was a heart attack. Why should I believe any different? Why should I ask? You were a kid of seven. I was a kid of seventeen. Same difference."

"She was, what, forty? Pretty young for a heart attack, no?"

"Maybe. I don't know. Things were different then. They didn't know what they know now. The signs ... symptoms. The tests. The procedures. My dad, I think, said something about heart problems ran in her family. I never knew much more about them. She came over from England on her own to work in the hospital. Anyway, What stories? When? From who?"

"Oh, you know, the sorts of stories kids tell each other over cigarettes and beer, sitting in abandoned buildings, jerking off with the wind rattling the windows."

"Ghost stories."

"Sure, why not? Apparitions of former patients haunting the hallways. Strange sounds. Tales of a woman in a nurse's uniform you can sometimes see on particular stormy nights who's swinging by her neck from a rope in the basement."

"You ever see her yourself? With your own eyes, I mean?" The old man looks at Ray who doesn't answer. "Me neither. I worked in the place for almost thirty years. I witnessed some frightening sights. Never anything of the supernatural variety, not even remotely. Anyway, two years after my mom, my dad was killed in a car crash. That was that. If there was anything suspicious, he took the details to his grave. I pretty much replaced him at his job as an orderly in the hospital and went on with my life."

"But grandma was a nurse there, right?"

"Yeah. That's where they met. My dad had been a patient since the age of six and when he turned nineteen, they offered him a job as an orderly. He took it. Some people might find that strange, I know. You'd think he'd want to get the hell out after all those years. Then again, what else was he fit for? And jobs were scarce, so ..." He shrugs.

"He was a patient?"

"Not exactly a patient. A 'ward' is maybe better. He was orphaned as a boy and nowhere to go, so they put him in the hospital. Happened a lot. Not unusual. He didn't talk about his time there as a boy except to say it opened his eyes to the world in ways that weren't entirely pleasant or agreeable or fair."

"Sounds ominous. He say anything else?"

"That was it. He wasn't much of a talker as I recall."

"Uh-huh." Ray tugs a handkerchief from his pants' pocket and wipes his face. "Aren't you cooking in this heat?"

His dad's clothed in a long-sleeved lined flannel shirt over a heavy grey cotton undershirt, grubby blue jeans with the pant legs tucked into thick winter socks and beat-up leather work boots.

"This? This is the sun you're talking about." He spreads his arms, drops his head back, stretches his face and rolls his tongue out. He inhales deeply through his nose. "Ahh," he says. "Solar energy. Manna from God. Onto the skin, through the pores, straight into the bloodstream. Recharges the batteries. Natural source of Vitamin D. Kills germs and bacteria. Wards off the evil spirits."

"Right." Ray tucks the hanky.

"Smoke?" his dad asks and produces two *roll-your-owns* and a Bic lighter from a wooden cigar box at his feet.

"No thanks. I quit."

"Since when?"

"Few years back."

"Howcum?"

"Don't know. Woke up one morning and somehow dis-covered I'd lost my taste for it. Tossed the remainder of a package in the garbage and that was it."

"Huh. That was it? Not much of a story."

The man lights up and hacks and wheezes for a good few seconds. Ray waits to see if anything comes up. Like a lung.

"No, sorry about that. I could spice it up a bit if you want. Add a few schmaltzy details. Personal revelation and so on. Death of a friend from the Big C or whatever. Make it more interesting." Ray tips the bottle enough for a splash of beer to hit his lips.

"Too late, forget it. How's the beer?"

"Like horse piss."

"It's an acquired taste. You don't have to finish it on my account."

"It's okay. It's cold and wet, which is all that matters."

"Suit yourself."

Ray rolls the bottle across his forehead. A crow helicopters down from the sky. The men watch as it lowers its claws and flutters a soft landing on top of a weather-worn fence post. Ray's dad tops up his plastic cup. He inhales a chest full of smoke and exhales through his nose with a moan. He taps the ash from his cigarette.

"Yep," he says. "Flat as bird shit on the hood of a Buick."

The pair sit there, hardly moving, and stare out over the prairie.

Give it a minute, thinks Ray. He's got more questions for his dad and all day to ask them. Let the old man finish his cigarette. No need to rush. Slow and steady wins the race, they say. Fine. He splashes the last of his warm beer on the ground and sets the bottle off to one side. He drums his knees with his hands. The two men slowly turn their heads to face each other.

∿ "Nightmares? What sort of nightmares?"

Beth stands in the kitchen rocking Casey in her arms. Ben sits at the table drinking coffee from a mug that reads: ~~Weyburn's~~ *World's* Best Dad.

"Sorts of things a baby shouldn't hear."

"What? You're joking, right?" She looks at Ben. "You're worried discussing Ray's nightmares will corrupt our child, is that it? Turn her into a sex-crazed, drugged-out, axe-wielding monster or something? A freaked-out, blood-thirsty, serial killer. Like she's even capable of understanding." Beth laughs.

"I'm just sayin'." Ben cocks his chin. "Remember the nurse telling us the foetus hears things in the womb that it starts to recognize and react to. By the time a baby's born, it's already familiar with its mother's voice. Recognizes it out of a group. Who knows what else?"

"If that's the case, Casey'd be humming Miranda Lambert tunes—*well the road was hot and flat as a ruler, good hundred miles between me and Missoula*—'cause that's who I listened to the entire time carrying her. Even through the terrible break-up with Blake Shelton. Cheating bastard."

"Still. I'm uncomfortable."

"That bad? Okay, I'll put her in the playpen." Beth hustles into the living room, sits Casey on the mattress, rattles a few toys, makes a few funny faces and gurgle-y baby sounds, and returns quick as a shot.

"Ready," she says.

"Where's Ben junior?"

"In his room playing trucks. Safe and sound. C'mon, spill already. Ray and his nightmares."

"Okay. Fine." Ben sloshes coffee around in the mug. "One nightmare in particular keeps coming back, he says. He's younger—a boy—and he's lying on a narrow bed, like a cot, or a stretcher, surrounded by large, beefy men. Some of the men are in starchy white uniforms. Others are in grimy work clothes or rags. Their faces are distorted, animal-like. He says the dream is so vivid he can smell the men. The greasy sweat on their bodies; their rancid breath. They tell him to behave himself, do what he's told, and he'll be okay, otherwise ..." Ben pushes at his mug. Beth pulls a chair up and sits next to him. "Ray says he can't move. It's like he's strapped down. The men start touching him. He can feel their hands and fingers moving over his entire body—probing, poking and prodding—stroking his hair, caressing his skin, fondling him. His private parts."

"That's terrible."

"Yeah. It gets worse. He imagines them placing their limp or their erect penises on his face, in his mouth, giving them blowjobs. He wakes up gagging. He's in tears and feeling sick to his stomach. Sometimes he even vomits."

"Oh, my God." Beth places a hand on Ben's. "Can any of that be true? I mean, do you ever remember any of that being done to you? By anyone? A relative or someone? A neighbour? My God."

"No, never."

"Did he ever mention anything? Say anything to you about this when you were growing up? I mean, how could he keep a thing like that to himself? For all this time? He couldn't."

"That's the thing, he never said a word to me about anything like this. And when I asked him if he remembers—truly remembers—if any of this *in fact* actually happened to him, he says no, he can't. Not a hint, not a glimmer."

"Trauma can cause that, right? A person to ... What? Repress memories of certain horrible events or experiences?"

"That's true. But he denies it completely. Says he's positive it never happened to him; says in some weird way, it's more like he's reliving someone else's nightmare. Like he's *there* going through the ordeal, but he's also observing it from a distance, from a slight separation."

"Out-of-body experience, you mean? Maybe he saw something on TV or read it in a book."

"Yeah. Or heard about it from someone else, forgot about it, and now something's triggered it to run over in his mind as being an actual part of his life."

"Wow! Sounds totally awful, whatever it is." Beth tilts her head to check on Casey in the next room. She's playing happily with a stuffed teddy bear.

"Yeah." Ben stretches his lips and grinds his teeth. "Y'know, that said, I do recall Ray behaving peculiar shortly after mom had gone. He was maybe eight or nine. Out of the blue one day he started to only wear the same single set of pyjamas with a cowboy pattern on them that mom had bought for him, specially ordered from the Sears' catalogue. I mean, we—dad and I—knew he loved those pyjamas, but now, for whatever unknown reason, he refused to wear any other clothes. Day after day he wore them. And not just at home in bed at night, but 24/7: outdoors, shopping, school, the works. Dad couldn't get them off him even for a wash. There was no talking to him about it. He'd thrash and scream and cry like a banshee. It was scary. Dad eventually gave up trying and let him be. Said what else was there to do? He could've hit Ray square between the eyes with a length of two-by-four and it wouldn't matter." Ben clenches and unclenches his fists. "Another thing. He couldn't wear a belt or a watch. Nothing tight. You couldn't strap him into the car seat. He wouldn't wear socks or shoes with laces; it was rubber boots or slip-ons or flip-flops. This lasted about a year, right through the winter."

"Huh. Weird. Did he see a doctor?"

"Oh, sure. Any number had a go: GP, paediatrician, child psychologist, psychiatrist. Lots of hypotheses about what may or may not be going on, but nothing anyone could nail down with certainty, never mind treat. Finally, they said it was likely a phase he was going through, and it might pass. Otherwise, wait and see if it gets worse."

"A phase? Doesn't sound very clinical to me. Or reassuring for that matter. In fact, I think if I was the mom, I'd be scared half to death."

Ben inhales and Beth is aware of a noticeable shudder that runs up his spine. She puts a hand on his back and strokes him.

"What is it? What are you thinking?"

"Something I remember. Something I can't forget, really. There were several nights where we'd be in bed sleeping—or I'd be sleeping, he was obviously awake—and he'd grab me by the arm, give me a rough shake, put his mouth to my ear and whisper to me ..."

Ben looks straight at Beth. He coughs to clear his throat. She can barely sit still.

"Yes? And what did he say? What did he tell you?"

"He told me he didn't want to live anymore. That he wished he was dead."

"Oh, my God, Ben." She rubs his back with a firmer hand, up and down, back and forth, across the shoulders.

"He was only a kid and he said this. I mean, what the hell? Where does an idea like that come from, y'know?"

"I know. It sounds impossible. What did you say?"

"What could I say? Nothing. I was maybe seven. I was scared shitless. I just lay there. Oh, wait! Another thing I remember distinctly those times he shared this with me: His voice was different in some horror movie kind of way. It's hard to explain. It was like he was possessed. Like it wasn't him speaking. When he was done telling me this, he'd just roll over to his side of the bed and go right to sleep." He snaps his fingers. "Like that."

"Sounds like something out of *The Exorcist*. Then what happened? I mean, something must've changed, 'cause ..." She scrunches her face and lets the statement hang in the air, looking for an ending.

"Don't know." Ben shrugs. "Like I said, about a year later, one fine spring morning, it stopped. Most of it, anyway. He never mentioned to me again about not wanting to live. He traded wearing the cowboy pyjamas for a clean set of clothes, including socks and a pair of laced sneakers. He still didn't like to be strapped into a car, which explains his favouring motorcycles, I suppose. If ever dad asked him why the change, he'd look at him like he had two heads. Like it never happened. Like the entire incident was totally erased from his mind. Maybe the doctors were right, maybe it was a phase. What type of crazy phase, I don't know. I guess we all sort of forgot about it after a while."

"Huh. Anything else? Dream-wise, I mean."

"He told me sometimes he dreams that he wakes up and there's this miniature figure of the devil perched to his left on the bedpost. It doesn't move, doesn't speak to him, just stares at him blankly."

"What can that mean?"

"I asked myself the same question, so I Googled the image back at the office. According to the various sources, devils in dreams sometimes suggest you may be holding on to negative thoughts about life, thoughts that have been affecting your mental health and bringing you down. It can also mean you're guilty of particular actions and repressing the guilt out of fear of punishment, and this hidden secret is harboured in your subconscious. Can also mean you're struggling with issues of morality."

"Can't say I've ever seen that side of Ray. Just the opposite, in fact. What did you say at the time? When he told you? Anything?"

"I told him, next time he has that dream, look over to the other bedpost. It'll be the figure of God there to protect him."

Beth's eyes widen and her mouth drops. "Oh, Ben, you didn't? How'd Ray react to that?"

"He gave me the same pathetic look you give me when I go there with you, which is rarely, right? To give myself some credit, I don't push."

"Uh-huh."

"Uh-huh. Then he asked if I'd gone and turned all religious on him. I told him no, not exactly, but I do believe in God. I have to. Otherwise, I can't see any reason to continue. I mean, what point would there be? To spend seventy or eighty years on this earth, do a job, raise a family, and then, nothing? It didn't make sense. If there's no God, no chance for eternal life, might as well toss civilization out the window and behave like animals. Dog eat dog and be done with it."

"Oh, Ben." Beth tries to contain herself, then can't, and breaks into uncontrollable laughter. She can hardly breathe.

Ben smiles and strokes her arm. "I'm sorry, Ben. I'm sorry. I love you, but ... when you talk like this ... I can't ..."

"I know, Beth. It's okay. I understand. We're different that way. I generally keep it to myself, you know that. It's just ... Ray seemed so ... down. I had to say something. It was all I could think of. Besides—finding God—it helped me."

Beth takes a deep breath. "Whoo!" She wipes the laugh tears away with the back of a knuckle. "It's okay, Ben. Sometimes you can't help yourself. What did Ray say to that?"

"The usual. That more people have been killed in the name of God, King and Country than any other reason in the world. Next to love, maybe. Said why is it, if someone believes in ghosts or aliens, they get tossed in the nut house, but if you attach the word 'God' or 'religion' to the same belief, it's okay? Said if people wanted to believe in delusions and bow down and pray to symbols, graven images, sacred golden calves, voodoo dolls, lucky rabbit's feet, or whatever, that's fine. They should just be forced to confine such intimate behaviour to the privacy of their own homes, same as masturbation."

"Ouch! He said that? A bit harsh. But, that's Ray. Calls a spade a fucking shovel. At least he sounds like he's given the subject some serious thought."

"I guess."

"Hold on." She holds up a hand. "I'm just gonna check on Casey. Make sure she still has all her fingers and toes. Back in a sec." She flies out of the kitchen. In short order, she's back in her chair, leaning forward with her arms on the table. "All good. What else?"

"He said something"—Ben twists his face—"odd. I don't know if he was joking or not. He looked me straight in the eye and said: if God is everywhere, then automatic store doors should always be open. Since they're not, it proves God doesn't exist." He drinks from the mug and runs his tongue across his lips. "He never cracked a smile, as if the argument made perfect sense to him, *quad erat demonstrandum*." Ben plays follow-the-bouncing-mug to draw out and underline the Latin.

Beth finds Ben's reaction slightly amusing and lets him know. "I'm sure he was pulling your leg."

"I don't know. The way he said it. It was eerie. Deadpan."

She leans closer and touches a palm to his cheek.

"Uh-huh. Well, I don't know. How about you? You okay?"

"I just want to help him."

"That's you in a nutshell," she says. "Face it, sometimes you can't. Some people, you can't. Remember that joke?" Ben gives her a quizzical look. "Wife tells husband about the work-associated problems of the day. So-and-so did such-and-such and what's-to-be-done? Husband tries to console and help by offering suggestions on what to do, how to handle. Wife suddenly gets angry, goes berserk, screams at husband, says she *knows* what to do, that's not why she's telling him. Husband is confused and asks, then what? Wife says, when I tell you my problems, as my husband, your job is not to try and fix the problems. Your job is to listen patiently, agree with everything I say, and otherwise shut the fuck up."

"It's more an anecdote than a joke."

"Tomato, to-mah-to ..."

"Uh-huh. So, as my brother ..."

"Listen, agree and shut the fuck up. He's a big boy. He'll figure it out."

"Yeah. Maybe I'll try that. But it's killer." He takes his mug to the sink and gives it a rinse. "I see you dragged the treadmill out of the closet."

"Yeah. Figured it's time to get back in shape."

"Nice. If you need help with anything ... equipment, setting up a routine ..." He turns his head and their eyes lock. Both grin.

"Never mind," he says. "I'm sure you can manage on your own."

Beth makes like a goofy bobblehead. "Yeah," she says. "I'm good. But I'll holler if I need you, okay?"

"Okay."

∿ "Your mom and dad, were they part of the drug experiments that went on at the hospital?"

His dad haws a low chuckle and pours himself more wine from the three-litre jug at his feet.

"*To make this trivial world sublime, take a half a gram of phanerothyme*," he quotes, using a circus barker voice.

Ray follows suit. "*To fathom Hell or soar angelic, just take a pinch of psychedelic*. So, you knew about the drug use."

"Jesus, Ray, c'mon. It was common knowledge. Written up in some of the best medical journals in the world. There was no secret, no cover up. It was totally legit at the time and an accepted medical procedure. All over and done with by the time I started. Yesterday's news."

Ray researched the history of the Souris Valley Mental Health Hospital and was aware that Dr. Humphrey Osmond, known as *The Psychedelic Psychiatrist*, experimented with LSD in the 1950s to the 1960s as a cure for chronic alcoholism with positive results. He also administered the drug to the medical team as it helped mimic particular states of consciousness that the more florid psychotic patients experienced. The idea was to gain a clearer understanding of these states and in so doing, create a more level playing field that would allow for an empathic bond to grow between the patients and the health professionals. That was the theory. There were other drugs being tested as well, Ray recalls. He doesn't remember the names, though one was affectionately referred to as "the spirit molecule."

What his dad said was accurate and correct. It was a new field, medically speaking, and the entire venture was considered scientifically sound and valid as well as important, even necessary, health-wise. Interest in Dr. Osmond's experiments went far beyond Weyburn, even beyond the boundaries of North America. Aldous Huxley visited from England and was provided with a dose of mescaline. His experience led to his writing the book, *The Doors of Perception*. It was he who invented the word "phanerothyme" to depict the impact of mind-altering drugs in his written correspondence with Dr. Osmond. By the seventies, these drugs were being phased out in favour of other treatments as large hospitals such as Souris Valley were being deinstitutionalized and eventually shut down.

"Your mom and dad, though, they'd've been in the thick of it. She was a nurse and was likely given some type of mind-altering drug, yes?"

"I suppose. I don't know. They never talked to me about their work."

"You don't recall anything?"

The man shakes his head. "All I remember is that before she died, she was seeing a doctor for something. They said it was mood swings. What did I know? I was busy chasing my own tail."

"Yeah." Ray hangs his head and scratches the ground with his boot heel.

"I'm not much help."

"It's okay." Ray stretches his back and rolls his shoulders. "To be honest, I'm not sure what I'm looking for or what I expect to find." He stops his action mid-way and his face takes on a puzzled appearance, as if struck by something.

"Huh," he says.

"What?"

Ray cocks his head and shoots his dad a look. "You just said that your mom had mood swings, yeah? And earlier you told me that *my* mom had medical reasons to account for her behaviour. What behaviour and what reasons?"

The man sucks his cigarette down to his tobacco-stained fingers. "She had a rough childhood. An orphan, part white, part Cree. No secret there, right? The Cree part, you knew about. Couldn't hide that. Not that we tried. Her skin, her hair. Not sure which part was mixed—mother, father —" he uses his hands like scales, measuring—"or how much from either side. Anyway, what you might not know is, she was bounced around from family to family. Physical and mental abuse from all sides. Pregnant at sixteen, who knows by who or under what circumstances, she never said. She had a miscarriage—thank Christ in my opinion, 'cause who knows …—followed by a complete mental breakdown. She ended up in hospital. That's how I met her."

"Wait a second—mom was a patient at Souris?"

"Yeah. Why?"

"Your dad was a patient at Souris, then an orderly. Your mom was a nurse. That's where they met. Same as you and mom, only the reverse. That never struck you?"

"No, should it?" The old man's face brightens, and he roars. "Ha! You think it's like some kind of, what ...? Supernatural occurrence? Maybe an omen? Or Karma? C'mon, Ray, get a grip. The two situations were decades apart. They had nothing to do with each other. Pure coincidence. Besides, there were lots of stories like that. Relations between patients and between patients and staff. *And* doctors. One doctor I was familiar with eloped with a patient. The brass did their best to keep the various sides apart, but it was next to impossible. There was always something. Patients escaping to be together and getting rounded up in town. I remember one such incident where a couple managed to hop a train and get as far as Regina before they were collared and hauled back. Turned in by a relative, in fact. So much for family ties and obligations." He laughs again. "You better check next time what's in the water you're drinkin'."

Ray flips his bottle across the yard and runs a hand through his hair.

"Don't look so disappointed. I told you. There's nothing to tell beyond the ordinary. Your mother went through some sort of odd moods after she had you and Ben. What her family doc called postpartum depression. Said it would pass, just keep an eye open. Right. Likely even a touch or two of bi-polar, if you ask me. She'd have days where she'd be over the moon happy, then crash for days. She'd go on spending sprees. Buy stuff on credit she didn't need or would just give away to whoever for no reason. Even went out a got herself a tattoo."

"I sort of remember her like that at times. I don't remember a tattoo."

"It was right before she disappeared. A circle of turtles around her right ankle. For many native American tribes, the symbol's supposed to represent good health and long life." He drains his glass. "We know how that turned out in the end."

"She never got treated?"

"Back then was even worse than today. No one wants to admit they're crazy. And once you've been inside a mental institute as a patient, you sure as hell don't want to go back."

"Yeah. Understandable."

"I tried to get her to seek some professional help. She'd have no part of it."

"Uh-huh."

The old man sighs. "Listen, Ray." He removes his sunglasses and pulls at his face. His manner softens and his voice turns conspiratorial-like. He bounces the sunglass frame on the arm of the chair to make his point. "I've got something of your grandfather's hid away. A sort of diary, I think."

"A diary?"

"I think, yeah, maybe a diary. Or a journal of some sort anyway. I don't know."

"Have you opened it; given it a look-see?"

"No, I figured it was personal and none of my business. It's in a box among a few other items. If you promise me something, I'll let you have it."

Ray doesn't understand the aura of secrecy his dad is attempting to create, nor can he fathom why he'd want to bargain for a book he obviously has no interest in. Maybe it's all for show, he thinks. Maybe it's his idea of a joke. And what sort of promise can he be expecting? Fine. Whatever. If his dad's willing to toss him a bone, he'll take it.

"Sure. What's the promise?"

"Kill me." He reaches out his hand and clutches Ray's arm above the wrist. The man was sixty-six, going on eighty, but he still had the firm strong grip of a twenty-year old—the result of lifting dead weight bodies and transferring them between beds and wheelchairs for years. "I mean it. I'm nothing but a handful of dust. Not even. Blow me away."

"You're not serious."

"I am. I'd do it myself, but I don't have the guts. Promise me, Ray, and I'll give you the book. Maybe you'll find something in it. Something useful."

"I can't do that."

"You can. You're the only one. It's in you. You could do it and not even blink."

"Maybe I've changed. Did you consider that?"

"A leopard doesn't change its spots and a skunk doesn't lose its smell. Kill me, Ray. Do it. Hit me over the head with the flat end of a shovel. Anything. I don't care how, just promise me you'll do it. What do you say?"

"No."

"Why not? You don't care if I'm alive or dead. You only came by to pick my brain and I've been no help whatsoever. I'm through, Ray. I'm just an empty bag of bones taking up valuable space. My wife's gone. My grandkids are too afraid to see me. Ben visits me out of guilt and a wrong-headed sense of family loyalty. Beth puts up with me because she's married to Ben, that's it. You'd be doing me and everyone else a favour." He squeezes Ray's arm harder. "I'm begging you. Please. Kill me."

⁓ The gal behind the bar, early twenties, is a strapping, healthy-looking, big-boned, energetic friendly sort with bleached hair and hooped earrings. She loads a tray with drinks and passes the tray neatly across the bar to a server. Done, she shifts her attention to the new arrival, flashes a row of small white teeth, slaps her palms on the rail and leans forward. Her open-necked blouse reveals a modest amount of cleavage, the pose meant to be enticing without being vulgar. This is the thought that passes through Ray's head, at any rate. She chews a stick of gum. There's a name tag on her blouse that reads Lisa.

Ray sits at the middle of the bar counter, no one occupying the stools to his right, while two stools to his left is sat a skinny young kid worrying a napkin to shreds between his fingers.

"What would you like, hon?"

"Belgian Dark Strong Ale," he says. He wants to erase any trace of his dad's homemade brew.

She laughs. "Sure, hon, don't we all. How about a St. Ambroise Pale Ale, instead? It's the closest we got."

"Fine," Ray says. He figures she's a trifle young to be calling everyone 'hon' but he's experienced the practice often enough before and assumes it comes with the territory: the service industry. No matter what age the customer, treat everyone as equal.

The skinny kid presides over a food-stained plate and an almost empty pint glass. He lowers his head, digs deep into his pants pocket, fishes out bills and change that he totals to himself between his knees. The bartender's familiar enough with the posture and jumps in.

"How 'bout you, hon, another?"

"I don't know," the kid says. "I'm already pretty wasted. My girlfriend's coming by to pick me up soon. She like, lives just up the street. I mean, she's at work, now, personal secretary or something, but after work. I'm stayin' with her only until I get settled somewhere on my own. I'm askin' around, checkin' the ads and so on. I need somethin' I can afford, y'know? It's tough. I'm not from around here. I was surprised at rent for what you get downtown, which isn't much. I want at least a one bedroom. Plus maybe a den. Whatever. Some space to move around in, put my stuff, y'know?"

A clear case of verbal diarrhoea, Ray thinks. No such thing in his vocabulary as a simple yes or no answer. Also, no filter. 'Do you want another drink?' was the simple question asked. He's wasted, so everything becomes a story for the world to hear. Look at that. Pathetic. The kid has the bartender's—Lisa's—attention and doesn't let up for an instant.

"Anyway," the kid goes on, "I don't have a key to her place, not yet y'see. We still have to ... you know ... work things out. It's complicated. Whatever. Something to do with her parents and the landlord and her lease. I don't know the details. Timing's everything, right? That's okay, it's cool, I'm cool."

Lisa stands courteously nodding, while keeping up duties behind the bar counter. "Sure, sure," she says. "These things take time. I understand. Been there, done that, bought the freaking T-shirt. Me and my boyfriend"—she rolls her eyes—"you wouldn't believe how long. You'd think he was afraid I'd show up one night, use the key he gave me to get in, slit his throat and rob him. Like he owned anything worth stealing, haha."

Ray's convinced the two could go on like this forever and not break a sweat, except Lisa is obviously a pro, and, somewhat better equipped at the chit-chat game than the kid. Also, she knows when to cut the cord and get back to business. She gets to the heart of the matter, *zing*, like the proverbial surgeon's knife: deep cut, little blood.

"So?" she asks. "You want another or the bill or what?"

"I dunno," he says. "There's still some time. How much is a beer?"

"It's Happy Hour, hon. Canadian pints on sale for four bucks. Can't beat it with a stick."

"Yeah, I think can manage that."

"We also accept all major credit cards, not just cash. Just sayin'." She gnaws down on her gum, creating a few popping sounds.

"Yeah, my card's kinda maxed out at the moment. S'okay. My girlfriend when she gets here'll have more money. I just wanna make sure, in case. I'm kinda wasted," he snorts a laugh.

"Sure, sure, that's cool," Lisa says, who slips smartly aside, pours the two beers, and drops them, one in front of each man.

"Like I said, I'm pretty new in town." He starts up again. "Got here like a month ago. From Regina."

"You're from Regina?" Lisa asks, sounding interested.

Gotta hand it to her, Ray thinks. She plays light and loose. Able to multi-task. Keep up with the conversation, fill drink orders from servers, wipe down the bar, slice limes and lemons, rinse glasses. The place is reasonably busy at the surrounding tables and booths and she responds like a Zen master—*Zah!*—with total poise.

"No, I'm from Saskatoon originally."

"Saskatoon, wow!"

"Yeah," the kid beams. "You been there?"

"Me? No, never. I'm from Moose Jaw."

"Oh, yeah? What was that like?"

"Like it sounds." She makes a face and gives a big laugh. "Anyway, you were saying, Regina?"

"Right." The kid picks up the thread. "I was workin' in Regina."

"Uh-huh? Doin' what?"

Lisa drops her forearms on the bar and gives the kid another clear shot of cleavage. For a tip or for a thrill or for no particular ulterior motive whatsoever—maybe just her manner along with calling everyone 'hon'—Ray isn't sure. All he knows is, he's glad he's not a bartender stuck within a few square feet of real estate, victim to every sad-sack loser with a boring tale to unload.

"I'm a mobile crane operator," the kid says, almost proud.

Ray shakes he head like he can't believe it. Sonofabitch, he thinks. The kid hands her a card, even. Oh brother, enough already. He expects that the pair'll be exchanging family photos on their cells next.

Ray washes a mouthful of beer around between his cheeks, then drags a thin hardcover journal from an inside jacket pocket, slaps it on the wooden bar and opens it. The front-page states: these are the personal notes of Frank (Francis) Nowak. Love, Vicki, 1968. So, a small gift from grandma to grandpa, Ray supposes. A P.S. reads: Don't worry, I bought it cheap at the Church bazaar sale.

Ray can only imagine. He flutters ahead to view further pages. His initial thought? Grandpa died in 1972. That's four years that he was in possession of the journal and yet each page is pretty much blank except for a single, sparse, neatly printed entry—consisting of a handful of sentences, though generally less—at the top. For no apparent reason, he underlined the dates, as if this was important. The journal begins: January 1, 1968. 'Nothing too exciting to talk about really. The snow is falling. The cat's gone missing though I'm sure it will return when it's hungry.'

Christ! thinks Ray. This is painful. The man was obviously forced by his wife to get started. There's no other reason to record this shit.

He scans page after page. It appears that his grandpa was even more tight-lipped than his dad. It goes on like this, a journal of inanities. Weather seems to be a highlight. Mention of a trip. No details about the trip, simply: 'Taking the train to Winnipeg. A relative has passed.' A further entry reads: 'Returned home from Winnipeg. It was a fine funeral, though considerably hot.' The final entry in the journal says: August 17, 1970. 'Vicki has been laid to rest. May God bless her soul. It threatened to rain and, fortunately, it held off, for there were several friends and family in attendance.' Again, no details as to the circumstances around her death other than minor comments, such as: 'Vicki out of sorts today. May be the weather.' Or: 'Vicki suffering from another bout. Will see the doctor.' Or: 'Vicki in high spirits this week. Maybe we've seen the worst I pray to God.'

Ray closes the journal in frustration and pushes it off to the side, shovelling it on top of a pile of used newspapers. 'Another bout.' Another bout of *what*, exactly? It might as well be written in Martian. The kid is still bending the bartender's ear, though she, by this time, is giving clear signals she's got other things to do, which the kid is either missing or ignoring. Ray thinks missing, as the kid is one of those natural chatty types who's in love with the sound of his own voice and is otherwise oblivious to the concerns of others. Need to hit him over the head with a freaking baseball bat to get him out of himself.

Somehow the conversation gets around to the fact he's twenty-one and has a four-year-old daughter from a wife living in Swift Current. Ray does the math. Holy shit, seventeen! Who knows how old the wife was? Planned? Or a game of hide the salami gone horribly wrong? Ray guesses the latter. 'I'll only stick it in a little ways, I promise. I swear. I won't come inside you. Oops, too late. My bad.' Meanwhile, what's the deal with the new girlfriend? Did he fall off the back of a pick-up truck and land directly into her bed or what? The bartender manages to extricate herself and Ray knows only too well, the kid'll be onto him next—dog to a bone or shit to a shovel—he's the closest target and sitting alone. Ray isn't wrong nor is he long in waiting. He barely touches the pint glass to his lips.

"How's the beer?" the kid motions with his chin. "I was thinkin' I'd try it sometime. Saint whatever, I overheard." He waves a finger in the general direction of the bartender, who's keeping herself busy. "Canadian's cheaper, though, and I'm a bit ... you know ... wasted, so I wouldn't appreciate it. The difference, I mean. The taste."

The kid laughs and licks his lips with a thick tongue. His eyelids are at half-mast as he puffs and coughs his words.

"The girlfriend'll be comin' by to get me soon. We only just met. I'm new to town. Nice bar. Nice place. What I've seen. Weyburn. I've travelled around a fair bit."

"Uh-huh."

So far, no news Ray hasn't already picked up on the fly. He wonders if the kid's worth killing time with or not. Not that he has a choice by the looks of things. At least until the girlfriend arrives. If she does arrive. If there is a girlfriend.

What the hell and why not? thinks Ray. Can't be worse than spending time with grandpa's so-called journal. Who knows, maybe in the end there'll be a story worth listening to. Maybe the kid'll stop using the word 'wasted' all the time, which is getting a bit repetitive and boring. Maybe, though he has deep doubts on both counts.

∿ "Was workin' in Regina. Before that was Fort McMurray. I was there for the big fire. Had to get 'coptered out." He makes mouth noises and hand motions like a sloppy helicopter pulling away. "Sort of cool. Ever been in one?" Ray indicates no. "Sort of cool." He guides his beer to his lips and stops short. "I'm a bit wasted. Oh, well ..." He sips. "No one got hurt in the fire, which they figured was some kind of miracle. A couple people injured due to car accidents tryin' to leave town, otherwise." He shrugs. "Had to go back later to pick up my rig. Not a scratch on it. Bullshit luck is what I call that. Insurance companies are a fucking nightmare, right? Bastards. I'm a mobile crane operator." He hands over a card. "Run my own business."

"Uh-huh." Ray studies the card. It's all printed matter: name, occupation and cell phone number. Black and white. Boring as a roll of recycled toilet paper. "I gotta ask, what's a mobile crane operator *do*, exactly?"

"Sure." The question excites the kid and he perks up. "I got a flatbed truck equipped with a hydraulic crane that can travel around and do particular small jobs. Replace store signs mostly, though sometimes contract with a town to change streetlights or whatever. Even put Christmas decorations over windows or on rooftops."

"Big demand for that?"

"Oh, yeah. No problem findin' work. And the pay's good. I mean, Fort McMurray pay was phenomenal." He whistles. "But ... s'okay. I put the word out here in town. Got a job to do for a guy tomorrow, which is good. Gotta start makin' some money quick. You got kids? No? I got two daughters aged four and two. Great kids."

Two, thinks Ray. He didn't learn to keep it in his pants or at least slip a glove on after the first one?

"I heard you say to the bartender you had a daughter. In Swift Current, yeah?"

"I told her that? Huh. Fuck. I'm pretty wasted, I guess. I don't remember."

"No problem, we've all been there. Wasted, I mean, on an afternoon. So, you've got two daughters and a wife in Swift Current. What happened that you're here and not there with them?"

"Oh, you know, same ol' same ol'. The only reason we got married was because I got her in the family way"—he flips a hand in the air and makes a weak guilty smile—"and I stepped up as the only manly honest thing to do. We tried to make a go of it together. Didn't work out in the end. We're still friends though. No hard feelings. She's living with her folks. I send money every month like fucking clockwork." He smacks the flat of a hand into the palm of the other. "I ain't no dead-beat dad, just so you know. I don't shirk my responsibilities, no way."

Friends, my ass. It's a scenario that's an age-old recipe for disaster. Just add a couple of short years, maybe even months to the "still friends" scenario and stir. Sooner or later the shit hits the fan. The ex'll be up to here with raising two kids on her own and the parents will be worse. Well, not my problem. He'll find out soon enough for himself, thinks Ray.

"Except you're not around to help out and watch them grow."

"I visit regular. As much as I can. 'Course, it's hard since if I don't work, I don't get paid and if I don't get paid ..."

"Vicious circle."

"Fuckin' *A*, brother."

"How'd you decide to be a mobile crane operator?"

"Same as my old man. Been doin' it all his life. He got me in. He paid for me to get my training and got me on with someone to do my apprenticeship, even helped me finance my own rig. Now I'm set."

"You plan to do this forever?"

"Sure, why not? It's all I ever wanted."

"You might change your mind. Thirty or forty years until you retire is a long time doing the same job over and over."

"Oh, I'm never gonna retire. By time I pay off what I owe my dad and the bank and the kids and likely more kids and so on, I figure I'll have to keep workin' until I die. Maybe after." He laughs.

"Uh-huh. And how's the girlfriend with all this? Does she know about the wife and kids and such?"

"Sure." He wags his head excited-like, up and down. "I told her up front and she's totally cool with it."

"Wow! That's great. Sounds like you got it made in the shade, my friend. I wish you luck. I gotta take a whiz, then meet up with some friends. You take care." Ray hops off the stool and exits to the john.

"Yeah, yeah. You too."

The kid sees the journal sitting on the bar and he picks it up. He goes to say *hey!* but Ray's disappeared. The kid has a backpack at his feet, and he casually slips the journal into a zippered compartment.

Ray stands at the urinal. What did the kid say? Being a mobile crane operator is all he ever wanted? Holy fuck! Ray reckons he'd rather put a bullet through his brain than live that kid's life. To each their own, I guess ...

He takes his time in the john, hoping when he returns to the bar, the kid'll be gone. Though he wouldn't mind a peek at the girlfriend just to see if she fits any stereotype—pick a favourite—or if she's somewhat of a surprise, pleasant or otherwise. He looks in the mirror. He can't help but envision a future filled with an army of skinny, young, horny mobile crane operators crossing the country, willy-nilly, impregnating the female populace at large, creating further armies of skinny, young, horny mobile crane operators and so on and so forth. Meanwhile, so much energy and print wasted in the false hope that we can depend upon the next generation of children to save the world from itself.

Yeah, right, says Ray, under his breath. Now pull the other leg.

He strolls along the hall and rounds the corner into the seating area. The stool where the kid sat is empty and the counter area has been cleared and wiped down with a rag. All evidence of him gone: *Poof!* Just as well. Any further conversation between the two and Ray may have throttled the kid as a public service.

⌇ The evening passes shooting pool and drinking beer, interrupted by bad karaoke and worse stand-up comedy. Around eleven o'clock a middle-aged female DJ takes the scene, dressed in full cowgirl regalia: snakeskin boots, jeans, woven leather belt with a brass horseshoe buckle, red and white chequered blouse, bolo tie, Dolly Parton makeup, curly red hair topped by a brown Stetson hat. She introduces herself in that ingratiating homey manner that seems to accompany such local attractions and proceeds to spin a mix of hokey new country tunes and seasoned chestnuts—Texas two-step to line dance—in order to accommodate the obvious generation gap that makes up the crowd. It's a tried-and-true formula and folks hit the dance floor in short order. As for Ray, he finds the choice of music overly schmaltzy and banal for his taste; more irritating than entertaining. He'd prefer to hear broken-voiced Lucinda Williams wail *Righteously* or Neil Young growl out *Powderfinger.* He decides to gather his gear and vacate the premises. It hasn't exactly been a day to celebrate in terms of discovery and revelation. In fact, it's been a total dud.

He mutters a tune—*look out mama there's a white boat comin' up the river*—and does a slight quick-step dance shuffle across the parking lot for the hell of it. Partway he notices the streetlamp over his bike is out. Could use the kid and his crane right now, he jokes. Replace the bulb and *voila!* Let there be light! Ah, well, he says, insert tab A into slot B, turn the key—all will be revealed. He realizes he's talking aloud, complete with tiny hand movements for emphasis. That's okay. The beer has served to take off the edge and he's feeling mellow, even relaxed. Not drunk, he tells himself. I never get drunk. Why is that? I have a capacity, a tolerance. Able to hold my liquor. What's the joke? How does a Frenchman hold his liquor? By the ears, haha! Would be nice though, sometimes. Lose myself in a bottle. Be someone other than. Who?

He reaches the bike. Quickly, from out of the shadows behind, a pair of thick, smooth brown arms surround him, pin his elbows to his sides and lift his body off the ground rendering him more or less helpless. A second figure appears dimly in front of him.

"I said watch your back."

"Barry, buddy! Whassup, pal?"

"You're up ... pal ..."

Barry rears back and drives a fist into Ray's stomach. Then a shot to the ribs, another to the shoulder, another to the face. Ray curls his body as much as possible raising his knees to attempt to block the blows, kicking out with his feet. Ki has a difficult time of Ray's thrashing and squirming and heaves him smack on his tailbone to the pavement. Ray goes into foetal position and Barry puts the boots to him followed by more jabs to whatever parts are available. A voice shouts from somewhere on the other side of the lot.

"Hey! What's going on?"

Barry gives a final shot to the temple and Ray feels himself slip into a half-sleep.

"Hey! Hey!" The disembodied voice or voices again.

Ray can barely discern the nature of the shouts nor hear the clatter of boots race toward him as he loses consciousness.

The attackers make a hasty retreat into the shrubs and race off the property.

~ The call gets Ben out of bed and into his uniform.

"What's up?" asks Beth. Then, rapid-fire. "What's the time? Who was that?" She's not quite awake. "Where are you going?"

"Hospital. It's around midnight. Ray's in emerg, apparently. Nothing too serious. Roughed up, is all. I shouldn't be long." He kisses her on the forehead. "Don't worry. Go back to sleep."

Ben saunters the hallways, tipping his hat and greeting the various staff who point him in the right direction. He checks the room number and it's empty. An orderly gives him a high sign: this way. He finds Ray sitting on a couch in a waiting area, his face scratched, bruised and swollen. One eye is blackened. Ben collapses beside him and drops his hat on a knee.

"What's the matter? You didn't like the room or the service or what?"

"I'm okay. I'm ready to leave."

"You don't look okay. In fact, you look like shit. You know who did it?"

"Yeah. A couple of pussies."

"They did a job on you from what I can tell."

"Are you kidding? I've been beat worse than this by a Kiwanis Club bingo player."

"Since when did you play bingo?"

"I was there with a lady friend. She was into it. I was along for the ride."

"And?"

"Oh, you know, they called out a few numbers, I yelled bingo, for the fun of it. Seems these players were very earnest, almost religious, and what I did was similar to yelling 'Hi, Jack' at an airport. No sense of humour. Sacrilege. Criminal. Next thing I know I'm tumbled out of my chair and being dragged by the collar by a security guard across the fake-wood laminate floor, down the corridor, through the exit door, outside to the pavement, where I was set upon and clubbed repeatedly with the wooden handle of an umbrella held by one of the bingo enthusiasts, a brawny grizzled woman who must've been ex-military 'cause she gave me quite the skilled and intense working over before she was satisfied that enough was enough, and let me go. Much to the delight of the rest of the mad cheering onlookers who followed us out, I should mention. Note to self: There's no such a thing as an innocent bystander."

"Uh-huh. Interesting. In my background check, I never found a record of you being in hospital."

"Didn't go. I was rescued by a Florence Nightingale-type in the crowd who nursed me back to health at her place."

"I take it she wasn't the same lady friend you escorted to the bingo game?"

"No way. That psychopath was egging the bouncer and the umbrella lady along with the rest of the crowd. She may even have thrown a few punches herself. I wouldn't doubt it. Figured I got what I deserved and washed her hands of me then and there."

"Uh-huh. So, do I need to ask who did this to you tonight, or do I know?"

"You mean Tweedle-Dum and Tweedle-Dee? Yeah."

"You want to press charges?"

"Naw. Coupla good old boys letting off steam. They've had their fun. It's over. I'm happy to let it go."

"Yeah?"

"Yeah."

"'Cause I wouldn't want."

"Ben—water off a duck's ass. Really."

"You sure you're okay?"

"Sure, I'm sure. No serious cuts, no broken ribs, still got my teeth and the family jewels are intact. I'm good. Don't you ever notice? Guys like this? They tend to hold back. They're afraid to do real damage. It's not in their nature. I told you, a couple of pussies. They're probably home right now worried about me, hoping they didn't hurt me too bad, wishing they hadn't done it. That, and afraid the law's gonna come knocking. Let 'em stew in their in their juice. I just wanna get home and go to sleep."

"Okay. I'll talk to the doc to make sure."

"Yeah, yeah."

"Why don't you drop by the house tomorrow, around four. I want to show you something. Maybe have a beer or two."

"Sounds good. I'll be there."

∿ There's no let-up. It's another bright, clear, warm summer morning. A hawk circles the sky looking for breakfast.

A flock of birds pulse a cloud above a distant tight copse of low trees. Everything's peaceful. Ray lays back in the lounge chair and allows Tantoo to dab his face with a soapy cloth. She applies a poultice of her own concoction around his eyes and covers it with the cloth. She presses the cloth flat with her palms. The poultice feels warm and soothing. She puts a hand on his shoulder as if to say: Rest and wait, this will help.

He's in no hurry to go anywhere. In fact, he's at a loss. Every so-called lead has turned into a dead end. He lets his mind wander. All it does is cover the same barren territory over and over again, turning up nothing new. Ben wants to show him something—what? Maybe he should visit the old house, the old haunt, and take a look around. What did Ben say about his dad? Too many memories in the walls. Maybe those walls will talk to him. Meanwhile, there's Barry to take care of. And his fat friend. In good time.

Ray drifts to sleep. When he wakes, he tries to remember if he dreamed anything. There's nothing he can recall. Okay, maybe he's at a point now where he needs a pipe to bridge the gap; bring on the visions. He senses a presence beside him, breathing. He knows it's Tantoo. She gently removes the poultice and cleans the area with the damp cloth. The swelling appears to have gone down somewhat and there's less throbbing pain. Fantastic. He swings his legs onto the ground. Thanks, Tantoo, he says. He goes inside the camper trailer, reaches a hand into a small backpack, fishes out a cell phone and checks the time. Early yet. He rips off his soiled T-shirt, sprays deodorant on his pits and chest, pulls a clean black T-shirt over his head. The bike's waiting. He hops aboard and motors into town.

It isn't difficult to gather the information he's after. People have become more relaxed, less suspicious of him, for whatever reason. Maybe they're getting used to seeing him around. Maybe they heard he had his ass kicked by a local. Funny how that works. In fact, his bruised face seems to make conversation easier. There's something concrete to talk about, as in: Hey, Ray, what happened to your face? Walk into a door, haha? Why lie? Used it to try and stop someone's fist. Didn't work the first time so I tried again. And again. And again. Bad idea. He plays out the action, mock punches himself in the face, boom, boom, boom. Some people never learn, he says. Everyone laughs. Everyone chills. And so long as he keeps his questions spaced apart, keeps his manner general and friendly, allows people a chance to speak their mind, no one's averse to talking openly and at length.

〜 He follows the GPS on his cell to an address on a quiet, secluded stretch of road that still allows for large yards. There's not a neighbour within spitting distance. Which often doesn't mean a thing as some folks seem to have developed a sort of built-in radar with regard to sniffing out suspicious behaviour.

He glides his bike into the drive, tucks his cell into a saddlebag, sidles to the door and knocks. A woman answers. Ray recognizes her, despite the fact she carries an extra twenty or thirty unruly pounds on her once trim frame and her face has a saggy, haggard look to it. Her hair's done up in a gawd-awful unshapely bun held in place by a few bobby pins. A cigarette dangles from one poised hand. The years have not been kind.

"Oh, my God," the woman says. She plugs the cigarette into her mouth, drags smoke to the filter and lobs the butt past Ray's ear. "What happened to you? To your face."

"Hi, Suze."

"Did my brother do this to you? That sonofabitch! He said something to me, and I told him. Oh, my God, Ray. I am so sorry. Are you okay?" She reaches her fingertips to his face and halts midway; withdraws her hand almost instinctively, almost as if burned.

Ray droops his head like a forlorn beaten pup. "It's okay, Suze. I deserved it. Really. For the way I acted. It was a wake-up call, and I got to thinking, you deserve an apology. That's why I'm here. To say I'm sorry for what happened those years ago. Sorry I ran away. Sorry I behaved like a coward instead of a man. I hope you have it in your heart to forgive me." He smiles and looks her straight in the eyes. "There. I've said my peace. If you can't forgive me, if you still hate me, I understand and I wouldn't blame you. You'd have every cause."

"Oh, Ray, I don't hate you. I never hated you. Of course, I forgive you. And I appreciate you're coming by to tell me. I do. It's sweet. I'm the one who should apologize. Putting that pressure on you. No wonder you ran. Then, in the end ... turned out to be ... well ..." She sighs and smiles. "You look terrific, Ray. You really do. Even with ... I'm sorry. That sonofabitch. I'll kill him, I swear."

"It's okay, Suze. Barry was protecting his little sister. It's only right."

"Protect me from what?"

"He knew I wanted to see you and I guess he was afraid I might try to take advantage of you, in some way."

"Sonofabitch."

"I told him the last thing I wanted do was put myself between you and your husband and your kids, but ..."

"Son-of-a-bitch!" She draws the epithet out. "Of course. I'm happily married now. Things have changed. What we had is gone."

"Water under the bridge."

Suzanne takes a deep breath and sighs. Her eyes are slightly welling. She twists a crooked goofy smile.

"Good to see you, Ray. Really. You wanna come in, have a coffee? A beer? Stay a while? Talk? What've you been up to? I don't even know."

"I don't want to impose. Besides, what if your husband ...?"

"What? No. Don't worry. Donnie's driving long haul to Winnipeg and won't be back for days. This is the kids' afternoon to stay with friends. The mothers do a sort of swap to have time for themselves and not go completely stir crazy. They're gone until dinner. Come on in." She steps aside to allow him room.

Ray is only too well aware of her situation, having sniffed out the information earlier in his discussions with the locals. He shuffles his feet.

"Okay," he says. "Maybe one beer."

"That's the spirit." As Beth is closing the door, she takes a quick gander up and down the street. It's deserted. She automatically turns the lock.

⌒ Ben's located in the driveway, shirtless, in baggy khaki shorts and blue rubber flip-flops, oiling a squeaky tricycle wheel, working on a beer, when Ray cruises in off the street.

"Howdy, little brother."

"You made it."

"Said I would." Ray folds his sunglasses over the bike's handlebars. "Beer me." He drags his hair behind his ears. Beth joins the boys from inside the house.

"Hey, hey! Arrest this man for failure to wear a helmet on a motorcycle. Not to mention stupidity. You lookin' to get yourself killed, Ray?" She straddles the bike seat. "I don't think these are regulation goggles either. Officer?"

"If I was to arrest every person who didn't follow the bike laws—especially in summer—we'd have no room for the gunslingers, drug dealers and rapists." Ben grins and drinks.

"Uh-huh. Very cool shades, though, I have to admit." She reads the label. "Armani, nice. Don't tell me—they were a gift, right? From a special friend of the female variety?" She tries on the sunglasses. "How do I look? Stunning, or what?" She goes into model pose mode.

"Totally sexy," Ray says. "I especially like the oversized checkered shirt and the bunny rabbit slippers."

Beth gives him the finger. "I'll have one of those."

Ben cracks two beers and hands them over.

"*Salut*. You want chips and dip? I'll get chips and dip."

Beth charges inside. The brothers make small talk. News, sports and weather. Lying politicians. Chance of showers. What about them Jays?

"Hey, remember when dad took us on a tour of the Asylum?" Ray asks, seemingly out of the blue. "We must've been like eleven and nine or ten and eight."

"Oh, yeah," Ben says. "Most of it had been shut down already. It was like walking through the set of a horror film.

All the beds crammed together. Those tubs where they gave ice baths. The chairs with the straps for electric shock treatments. Creepy. And some of the stories of the inmates he told us about. 'The man who couldn't stop painting.'" Ben stresses the title in bold quotes with his fingers.

"Yeah," Ray says. "They gave him art materials and he went to work on the walls like a demon. Covered them with a mural. Dad said it was a depiction of the Regina Riot of 1935."

"That's right. Good memory."

"Uh-huh. I also remember that a former employee had written a poem on a wall in black felt pen. Also, creepy. What the hell did it say?" Ray squeezes his eyes shut and hums and haws. "Wait a sec! *No more cries and silent screams to echo in the night* ... Something, something. *The clocks have stopped* ... Something, something. *The lights are out* ..." He blows through his lips and shakes his head, stumped.

"Not bad. That's more than I remember."

"Imagine working there all those years surrounded by all levels of madness and bizarre behaviours and strange phenomena."

"I can't and I don't want to. I don't think I could stand it. Give me your everyday criminal-type or traffic violator anytime." Ben laughs.

"Didn't seem to bother dad, though. When they shut the place down and let him go, he was pretty pissed. He figured to retire there. Or die, I guess. Goes to show, you can get used to anything if you need to earn a living and raise a family."

"There but for the grace of God ..."

"I suppose."

The brothers stand there awkward and quiet. They stare over shoulders and tap the bottoms of their beer bottles. Ray tugs at the flesh on his throat. He grins and lets out a low chuckle. Ben turns to him.

"He asked me to kill him," Ray blurts.

"What?"

"Kill him. Thought you should know."

"Who?"

"Dad. Who do you think? I went out to see him and he asked me to kill him."

"Shit, Ray."

"I know."

"What did you say?"

"I said no, what do you think?"

"What did he say?"

Beth interrupts the conversation. She wears a pair of tight blue shorts, a white blouse with the top few buttons undone and skinny-strapped leather sandals. Her hair hangs loose. She drops the snacks on a small table and tongues a corn tortilla chip with salsa into her mouth.

"You didn't have to change on my account. I was merely being boyishly playful when I mentioned the shirt and bunny slippers."

"Huh!" Beth cuddles close to Ben. He rolls his arm over her shoulder. "Don't worry, I didn't. Time for cocktail attire, that's all. Prove we're not all smalltown savages, *drinkin' 'shine in our undies outta mason jars*." She gives the words a musical southern hillbilly spin.

"Okay," Ray says. "Got it."

"Your face doesn't look too bad considering what Ben told me. Thought it would be a helluva lot worse."

"Takes a lickin' goes on tickin'," Ray says, grinning widely. "Ow! Still a bit tender."

"Only hurts when you laugh, huh? Know how to cure that?"

"Don't laugh!" the trio says in unison. All laugh and all grimace in mock pain.

"Funny. Hey, Ben? You wanted to show me something."

"That's right." Ben unwraps his arm from Beth. "Over here." He leads Ray into the garage and hands him his beer to hold. There's a brown cloth tarp and he slowly, carefully, gathers it in folds.

"Oh my God!" Ray says. "Is that what I think it is?"

"Likely." Ben takes his beer. The two men drink and stare. It's an almost sacred moment. A moment replete with absolute awe, respect and admiration. "1981 Harley Davidson FXE 1340 Super Glide Springer. V-2, four-stroke, 4-speed."

"Say it again. Sounds like a mantra. It's incredible. Where'd you get it?"

"Unlike you, I have no capacity for taking indiscriminate parts and putting them together in a correct order. I saw an ad. Beth and I drove down to Wolf Point, Montana—with the kids, Casey being practically a newborn—where I bought it and drove it back into Canada."

"So, it runs."

"Like a top." The two continue to fawn over the machine. "I figured, maybe we take the bikes Sunday morning, not too early, do some fishing, come back to the house for afternoon BBQ. Toss the day's fresh catch on the grill. I got extra equipment, rods and such. Beth said she'll fix us sandwiches. I got beer and a mickey of the Captain. What do you say?"

"I generally jinx a fishing expedition."

"No sweat. We'll cook steaks if need be. Though I expect we'll be fine. Go to Nickle Lake. Walleye, Perch, Northern Pike."

"Speaking of dinner." Beth stands in the shadow of the garage door opening, like a silhouette, beer in hand, arms crossed, legs slightly parted, a hip jutted, her instep turned up causing her knee to bend inward.

She looks extremely foxy, think the men, without letting on.

"Are you staying, Ray? It's no problem. I can toss another wiener in the pot." She tips the bottle to her mouth.

"Yeah," Ben says. "Be happy to have you."

"I'd like to. Other plans. Sunday, though, fer sure. Speaking of which, I gotta get goin'. Appointment to catch. Thanks for the beer."

"How do you know, Ray? You don't own a watch. Or a cell. Could be five in the goddamn morning for all it matters." Beth returns to the chip bowl. "Or have you gone all native on us and able to read the time by the position of the sun?"

"Something like that, maybe."

Ray throws a leg over the bike seat, fires the machine up and noses it onto the road. Ben and Beth watch until he's out of sight.

"Why you wanna be so hard on him?"

"He gets away with murder, Ben. And everyone lets him. 'Cause he's good looking and personable. Sooner or later, though, the roof's gonna cave. He's in for a fall and who knows who he's gonna take down with him. I don't want it to be me and I sure as hell don't want it to be you, Ben. Do you understand?"

"Doesn't have to be that way, Beth. We can help him."

"No. We can't. But I expect you'll keep trying."

"And you?"

"Me? I'll keep my fingers crossed, that's it. But I'm not holding my breath it'll accomplish anything useful." Beth scoops another chip into the salsa and delivers it to Ben's mouth. "You gotta help me with these, otherwise I'll eat the whole bowl. You know what I'm like. It's the Polish in me." She dives in. "What do you think he has to do that's so GD important he can't stay for dinner?"

"Beats me. He's searching for something. I don't know what. I'm not sure he knows."

"Huh. I should see to the kids. They're building forts out of furniture and sheets. Hot dogs tonight, okay? And be careful in the sun, it's still hot enough to burn. Not to mention skin cancer. Did I mention skin cancer? You think 'cause you're one sixteenth or whatever Cree you won't burn? We have sunscreen."

She enters the house shaking her head, her voice trailing. Ben rolls the trike into the garage and replaces the tarp on the motorcycle. He lowers himself on the seat of his Bowflex machine and tries to put together the pieces of the puzzle that are Ray. Then there's the business about their dad. What's with that? Kill him? What the fuck is going on? Also, there's something about the poem Ray recalled written on the Asylum wall that troubles him, though he's not sure what. Something he can't quite put his finger on.

⌒ Parking lot of the local rec centre. Stars are out and there's a fingernail moon hooked in the sky. Ray remains out of sight, hunkered in a dark corner of the lot. It's times like this he appreciates the fact there are still folks who are creatures of habit, who live their lives according to fixed patterns and schedules, down to where they park their cars. There's a short beep and the lights flash on the SUV. Before Barry has a chance to open the door, Ray lunges and pulls a clear plastic bag over his head. He yanks the drawstring, winds it around the man's neck and pulls tight. Barry struggles and grabs at the bag and drawstring. No dice. He lets out a moan. Ray punches him hard twice in the kidneys. This pretty much empties Barry's lungs. His knees and legs buckle. Ray drags him into the bushes, gives him a few more rapid blows to the ribs and belly. He shoves Barry's skull into the dirt and hammers at his face. Barry's body goes limp. His arms lie uselessly at his sides. He struggles for air and as he inhales, the plastic wraps his face and fills his mouth. His eyes begin to bulge, his breathing grows shallow. There's no fight left, and Ray can see him losing consciousness. His head droops, his tongue lolls out the side of his mouth and his eyelids begin to shut.

Ray presses his lips up real close and personal. "Before you go nighty-night, arse-wipe, I want you to hear something." He slaps Barry's face to get his attention, then loosens the drawstring slightly so he doesn't choke to death. The man twists his neck, his eyes slowly open and he looks up at Ray.

He's all ears.

5.

*"No more the cries and silent screams
to echo in the night ... The clocks have
stopped ... The lights are out ..."*
—Margaret Strawford, 2005

t's a perfect morning for fishing. The sky is cloudless, the surface of the lake is calm and there's barely a breeze in the air. The pair are in a rowboat. Lines hang in the water and the rods are wedged under the seats.

"You don't own a pair of shorts and sandals?"

"I like jeans and boots. Makes for a quick getaway, if I need it."

"Guess that means you're not planning to stick around."

"And do what?"

"Work, why not? Lots of job openings these days. Weyburn, The City of Opportunity." Ben spreads his arms to the world. "Find a girl. Settle down. Raise a family."

Ray stares coolly across at Ben, his lips twitching. His words are measured and deliberate. "Little brother, I'd rather shove the barrel of a Glock between my teeth and pull the trigger."

"Uh-huh. Okay. I'll let it go. For now." Ben raises his sunglasses above his eyes and squints skyward. "Looks to me like the sun's over the yardarm. You ready for a rum and Coke?"

"Sure, why not? Like Jimmy Buffet says, it's five o'clock

somewhere. Another beer and I'll be pissing over the side. Probably a law of some kind against that, I bet."

"Yeah, there is." Ben mixes two cocktails from a small cooler. "Lime?" he asks. "Cuba Libre." Ray nods, sure, and Ben squeezes fresh juice from quartered slices into each glass. "Funny how little it takes sometimes to go from the plain to the exotic. Which reminds me and I've been meaning to ask." Ben sucks the rum through the ice cubes. "I bumped into Barry Leask yesterday outside the gas station. He had a similar shiner to you on his eye. Though, I must say, yours is clearing nicely. Can hardly tell."

"Uh-huh. I'm a quick healer."

"I asked him about it."

"What'd he say?"

"Said he walked into a door."

"Doesn't surprise me. Statistics show most accidents occur around the home."

"He appeared pretty sheepish. Would hardly look at me."

"Embarrassing, I wouldn't doubt. Wham!" Ray smacks his forehead with a palm. "And, so?"

"And, so ... I was wondering if maybe you had something to do with it? Rather than a door."

"Between you, me and the fence post? 'Cause I wouldn't want to call good old Barry a liar."

"Between you, me and the fence post."

"Yeah, I paid him a friendly call."

"Should I be concerned?"

"About?"

"I know he was worried you might have some notions with regard to his sister. Then there's Ki."

"Not to worry, that business is taken care of."

"Meaning what, exactly?"

Ray grins and chuckles. He laughs. Ben fake-chuckles along with him and motions Ray with his glass to please continue.

"Well, after I made sure that Barry was in a mood and in a position to listen to me closely ..." —Ray forms a fist— "... y'know? I told him I'd paid a visit to his sister's place earlier in the day. Told him she was very pleased to see me. *Very* pleased. Told him one thing led to another and the next thing you know, she had her soft sweet lips wrapped around my hard, stiff cock, sucking me off like a bitch in heat. Told him after that, I fucked her raw between the clean white sheets of her marriage bed. I said, think of that next time you talk to her. Her pretty, soft, sweet lips sucking my cock.

"I told him that later, after his sister, I tracked down his pal Ki and fucked him up the ass. The thing is, I said, he didn't resist. In fact, he enjoyed it. So much so, he begged for more. Ki likely wouldn't tell him, all things considered, but I thought he should know that his good, best buddy's a fudge packer. He might want to think twice next time they're lathering up in the gym shower together; be careful not to bend too far over to pick up the soap." Ray's almost doubled up. His sides ache. He takes a good, long swig of his Cuba Libre and smacks his lips. "The lime's a nice touch. I like it."

Ben puts on his best poker face. Like they're discussing shoe size. "I gotta ask Ray: did you? Did you do that to Suzanne and Ki?"

"C'mon, Ben. No way. I never laid a finger on either of them. I didn't have to. All I had to do was plant the seed in Barry's thick skull and let his small dirty mind do the rest. It'll eat at him, and eventually ..." He throws his hands into the air. "Easy. That's how it is, Ben. Human nature. People are always more willing to believe the worst of what they're told about someone, rather than the best. I don't have to have done half of what people think I did. They believe what they want to believe. Sometimes even if all the evidence proves otherwise."

"It's a sad state of affairs, if it's true."

"Tell me about it. Anyway, don't shoot me, I'm just the messenger. How about one of those sandwiches your good wife put together? I'm putting my money on tuna 'cause she thinks we're gonna be hooped as fishermen and return home empty-creeled."

Ben slowly unpeels Saran wrapped sandwiches.

"What did I read? That every year we make enough plastic film to shrink-wrap the entire state of Texas."

"Good thing we live in Canada. Ham and cheese on rye." Ben rips the top off a plastic container. "There's pickles. Homemade dills."

"Beth thinks of everything. She's a peach, Ben. You're one lucky man."

"Yeah." Ben reclines on his life jacket and folds his ankles over the edge. "I've been thinking about our conversation the other day. Remember after the Asylum shut down? Some theatre group went in and put on a play. The whole town lined up to see it."

"Oh, yeah." Ray bites into a sandwich and chews. "We both thought it was a piece of crap. Bunch of actors pretending to be staff and inmates."

"That woman standing in the middle of the room, flapping her arms in the air, talking to herself," Ben says laughing.

"Yeah—look at me, look at me, I'm mad! Ooooooooohh-hh ..." Ray does his version of a damsel in distress.

"The guy playing the doctor or the male nurse or whatever. He kept leaning out the window shouting: Keep it down, retards!"

"There was no one out there. Who was the retard? Meanwhile, there's this group marching up and down the hall playing musical instruments. What the hell was that supposed to be?"

"I know. And there were those huts in the rooms that they hired artists to create. They obviously never saw the real thing."

"Yeah, couldn't hang yourself in one of those if you tried."

Ben pretends to hang himself by tugging on an invisible rope, twisting his neck and sticking out his tongue. "Fucking artists, eh?"

"Unbelievable." Ray finishes his Cuba Libre. "Why'd you bring that up?"

"I don't know. Seems stupid now that we talked about it. I thought maybe you might have seen something there that stayed with you. Maybe caused some of these dreams you've been having."

"Don't see how. I think I laughed more than anything."

"There was that one gal though. Jumped out at us from a dark corner. Dressed in a nurse's outfit. Held a huge hypodermic needle. That was pretty freaky."

"I remember that. Except, it was a male nurse. Built like a gorilla. Must've weighed two hundred pounds or more. Had on a sweat-stained T-shirt. Thick hairy arms. Butt ugly."

"No, I'm pretty sure you're wrong. She was like Nurse Ratched out of *One Flew Over the Cuckoo's Nest*."

"I think I'd remember this guy. He grabbed me. I could feel his sweat on me. I could smell his stink. I can still smell it."

Ben bites his lower lip. "Maybe you saw this guy in another room, after we got separated for a time." He grunts, *huh*. "That's funny. You sure you don't remember the Nurse Ratched?" The pair study each other and Ray shakes his head. The memory's lost to him. "Okay, that's fine. Maybe it's me that's mistaken the movie for the play. Though I don't recall any gorilla." Ben snaps his fingers. "Oh, yeah, something else. That poem you recited the other day. It had me scratching my head 'cause I had no recollection of there being a poem on the wall when dad gave us that tour of the Asylum. None. In fact, thinking about us going to the play, I realized it wasn't on the wall then, either. So, I Googled it. The woman who wrote it put her name and the year underneath, 2005. So, you couldn't have seen it until you were at least seventeen."

"Is that supposed to mean something?"

"I don't know. Maybe. I'm just saying. I mean, you're trying to put things together, right? To try and make sense."

"Yeah."

"Yeah. I just think it's important to keep things in order."

"I hear you. You're right."

There's a sudden pull on one of the fishing lines.

"That's yours," Ben says, jumping. "You got something."

"Here, you reel it in." Ray hands Ben his rod. "I'm outta practice."

"Sure, sure." Ben grabs hold of the rod and plays the fish. There's not much fight; he brings it in easy. "It's a pike," Ben says. "Undersize." He unhooks the barb and tosses the fish back into the lake. The two men stare into the water as it wriggles and dives under.

"Ben."

"Yeah?"

"I want to go visit the old house. Take a look around."

"Sure. No problem. You won't find much and what's there is covered in dust and cobwebs. I've got a spare key at home. Remind me to give it to you tonight."

"Uh-huh. I think I've had it with fishing."

"Yeah, me too. We'll head back. Knowing Beth, she'll have the steaks marinating. To be honest, I'm not much of a fisherman either, considering our blood background."

Ben packs the gear neatly into a duffle bag. Ray handles the oars, leans his back into it and rows slowly to shore.

∼ The patio lanterns offer a nice, warm glow around the deck. Ben scrapes the BBQ grill with a wire brush while Beth and Ray mosey into a couple of deck chairs on the lawn and get comfortable. A ring of smudgy citronella candles burns to keep the mosquitoes at bay. The two sit back, drink beer and stare at the night sky. Bats perform their fluttery panto-mime, zipping in and out of view. Kathleen Edwards sings *The Cheapest Key* over the boom box. Beth picks up a lyric and directs it jokingly at Ray: *'B' is for bullshit and you fed me some* ... He grins and points both index fingers at her, like: *touché.*

"I'm going to clear the plates and make sure the kids are okay. Ben junior's watching *Toy Story 3* for the umpteenth time and Casey was napping last I checked, so I'm guessing all is well. You two entertain yourselves." Ben scoots past the lantern glow into the shadows. He flips the porch light on as he reaches the door.

"Sure, bud. Nice job on the steaks." Ray slides his tongue across his teeth. "Tasty."

Ben disappears into the house and Beth gets suddenly serious.

"I need to say something, Ray. There's something you should know. About Ben."

Ray cocks his chin in her direction. "Shoot."

"He comes across as calm and confident, and in many ways he is, but, he hasn't always been. He took it hard when you left."

"How so?"

"Some kind of depression, I suppose. He went all quiet. I mean, quieter than usual. For Ben. Took to driving out into the prairie nights to spend hours on his own."

"Doing what?"

"No idea. Maybe run around bare balls, howling at the moon. Wouldn't surprise me. Anyway, he saw a couple of doctors, took some medications, nothing really helped. Then he found God. Don't ask me how. He just did. And that seemed to settle him. It seemed to give him a sense of purpose and direction."

"Uh-huh. And you're telling me this because?"

"Go easy on him, that's all. He doesn't look it, but he's fragile." Beth scratches at the label on her bottle. There's a moment of uncomfortable silence. She sucks in a deep breath. "You ever curious about how Ben and I got together?"

"I just figured, after I left, the two of you sought solace in each other's company and one thing led to another."

"Wow! You make it sound so easy. With yourself as the common denominator."

"You liked me, why not like my brother?"

"Right, right. As if the two of you are cut from the same cloth. I gotta tell you, Ray, I don't know brothers who are so un-alike. Apart from the general appearance, I mean. Black hair, red earth skin, aquiline nose, otherwise ..."

"Otherwise?"

"What's inside you, Ray?" She gives him a soft punch in the chest. "Is there anything in there? Does anything affect you?"

"You mean, like a soul?"

"A soul?" Beth roars. "Let's not get carried away." She stomps her feet and jumps out of the chair. "Fuck it! Y'know? Forget about it! Forget I even mentioned it. I need another drink." She spots Ben returning. "Ben, honey, Cuba Libres, all around, yeah?"

"You got it." Ben does a quick reverse back into the house. Ray tosses his beer bottle onto the grass, pushes out of his chair and stands by Beth.

"Beth"

"It's okay, Ray, really. I don't know what got into me. I'm sorry. We're supposed to be having fun here and I'm acting like Debbie Downer. Hey, I've got a joke for you. Pick a number between one and ten. Go on."

"Okay, Beth, um ... three."

"Three? Did you say three?" She shakes her head. "No, sorry, three doesn't work. Pick another."

"Okay, six."

"Six? How did you pick six? That's crazy."

"What's crazy?"

"That's my number! How did you know that? That's my number. You can't have it. Pick your own number."

Ben arrives with the drinks. He's got a big grin on his face. He's familiar with the joke.

"Ben, he picked my number. Did you tell him?" She and Ben laugh. "You told him, right?" Ben shrugs, no. "Pick another."

"Four."

"Four? Four? What kind of a stupid number is that? Nobody ever picks four." Beth and Ben crack up, they can't stop laughing. She covers her mouth with a hand. "Anyway, Ray, I'll stop. It goes on like this until all the numbers are used. The person telling the joke says whatever the hell nonsense they want so it's a different joke every time." She tastes her drink. "Wow, strong! I like it. You're not laughing. I think it's hilarious. Don't you think it's hilarious?"

Ray looks more confused than amused. "It's kinda cute, yeah. It's not really a joke, though, is it?"

"That's what I said when she used it on me," Ben says, still laughing.

"Of course, it's a joke! What is it if it isn't a joke?"

"I don't know. I think it's more, a gag."

"Gag, joke, what's the difference?" Beth abruptly stops laughing and her attitude turns deadly grim. She huffs and squints squarely at Ray. She shoots a look at Ben, who starts to say something, thinks better of it, and zips his lip.

"I think a joke requires an obvious punchline," Ray says. "Part of the definition. Though, I'm not positive."

"A punchline? That's it? That's your fucking problem with my joke?" Beth spits the words and gives them the opportunity to hover in the air a while, maybe pick up some added force. Then she unexpectedly rips out a shriek and jumps up and down. "I'm fucking with you, Ray. Jee-zus!" Everyone relaxes. "I had you going, yeah? Both of you. Wham bam. That was fun. Gotcha."

She extends her arm and holds out her glass. The men follow suit, though raising their glasses tentatively, unsure as to what Beth plans to toast, but then they grin and clink anyway, like: what the hell!

"To family," Beth says. "Thick and thin and whatever else other bullshit comes along."

"To family," Ben says.

Beth smacks Ray on the shoulder. "Ya big goof! Anyway ... gag, joke, what's it matter? I think it's hilarious." She sighs. "And, for your information, the magic number is nine."

"Why nine?"

"Because it's always nine, silly."

"Uh-huh," Ray says. "Except when it isn't, yeah?"

"Exactly." Beth pops her lips. "Except when it isn't. You see? You got it. You understand."

⌇ When Ray arrives at the house, he notices the front door's open a crack. He pockets the key he was given, climbs the couple of steps and pushes inside. Hello, he says. Anyone home? The first thing that strikes him, the second if you count the open door, is that the interior is spotless and meticulously arranged. There's even a planted pot of daisies placed *just so* atop the low coffee table. Is it possible Beth drops by to keep the place in order? Ray wonders, though this seems unlikely, all things considered. He gives the air a sniff and is greeted by the aroma of fresh coffee. Hello?

He calls again. This time toward the kitchen. An elderly man shuffles his moccasined feet into the room. Mid- to late-eighties, at least, Ray reckons. Aboriginal, likely Cree. Dressed in faded blue jeans, chequered shirt, a beaded buckskin vest, a beaded leather headband decorated with a coyote motif, an eagle feather stuck in back. His grey hair is braided down to his waist. He flashes a bright, red-cheeked smile across his ruddy round face. The guy could pass for a First Nations' version of Santa Claus. Hello Ray, the man says, his manner gentle, articulate. Welcome. Sit down. Take the load off your feet. The man gestures with the half-sweep of an arm. Any-where. Ray cocks his head. Sorry, do I know you? he asks, and waggles his hands in the air, as if to invite more information. Unlikely, says the man. I'm an acquaintance of your dad. I don't say friend, as your dad never really had friends, did he? We worked together at the hospital. The name's George Kiche. I worked with your grandparents there as well, I've been around that long. I see, says Ray. What are you doing here? In the house. Ben never mentioned you to me. George claps his hands together and rubs the palms one against the other. It's simple, really. Your father no longer had a use for it, whereas I did. He said I could make myself at home, and I have, as you can see. As for Ben, I tend to come and go. Our paths haven't crossed. Coffee? George takes a half-step toward the kitchen. I'll pass, thanks, Ray says. Fine, George says. Something stronger? Depends, Ray says. What've you got? George takes a pipe from the fireplace mantle, strikes a handy wooden match and lights up. He takes a couple of puffs to get the contents of the bowl going. I understand you're looking for information about your family, he says, and passes the pipe. Yeah? I guess. Maybe. I'm not so sure anymore. I can't seem to find anything solid to hold onto. Nothing but shifting ground. I'm beginning to think a needle in a haystack would be easier. Ray inhales. You mentioned you knew my grandparents? Oh, yes, George says. During the time. The time? Ray asks. Of the drug experiments, of course. LSD and mescaline in particular. You're wondering about your grandmother, yes? How she died?

Where does this guy get off? Ray puzzles. How does he know so much about my business and what's his angle, if he has one? The story about him being here and Ben not knowing also sounds more than a little suspicious. Still, there's nothing that appears threatening about the man or the situation. A little odd, a little creepy, is all. Might as well hear him out.

The pipe's contents are already going to Ray's head and he squeezes his eyes open and shut to try and clear the cobwebs. Yes, he says, I ... George interrupts. There was no problem with the drugs, *per se*, if that's your concern. Everyone involved was extremely content and functional. It was only after the drugs were taken away that people began to suffer difficulties: hallucinations, delusions, and so on. Symptoms of withdrawal. Not everyone, of course, though your grandmother was one of several who did, unfortunately. She wasn't a unique case by any means. Those affected either learned to live with it or else sought treatment. Whereas your grandmother ...

The man could be a psychiatrist, thinks Ray, the way he talks: '*per se.*' Of course, he only said he worked with his dad and grandparents, he never said in what capacity and

Ray just assumed he was an orderly. Of course, he could as easily have been a patient and gained his associations and knowledge that way.

George takes a few deep puffs on the pipe.

What do you mean? What happened? What did she do? Ray feels his lips going numb and his tongue thicken. He mumbles his words.

Your grandmother was addicted and since no one would supply her with the drugs, she procured them in other ways. Either bought them from disreputable sources or else stole them from the hospital pharmacy. Unfortunately ... Ray's head spins. The world around him is getting thick and foggy. He rubs his temples with his fingertips. He does his best to focus and plough forward with his questions. Unfortunately, what? The words ooze from his mouth. He can barely hold himself upright. George taps the bowl's contents with a thumb, snuffing the glowing embers. He wraps an arm around Ray's waist and settles him onto the couch. He leans his face close to Ray's. Since no one knew she was taking the unauthorized drugs, he says, she was left unsupervised and unobserved. She took too much. Combined with her family history of heart problems, it caused an attack. An accident, really. Or an accident waiting to happen, if you like. It's all in your grandfather's journal. No, Ray protests weakly. It's not. I read it. There was nothing. No details. George straightens and steps away. He smiles, smug as a carved Buddha. There's another journal, he says. He nods slowly to allow time for his words to strike home. Ray's a crumpled mass on the couch. He tries to stretch his fingers and is unsure whether they move or not. Your father has it, George say, straight-faced. What he gave you was your grandfather's attempt to appease your grandmother and, finally, to protect her reputation. But there's a second correct and explicit journal. Not just concerning your grandmother, it includes particulars about the Asylum in general, not all of it favourable. Your father has it. He's read it. He knows the truth. The truth? What truth? Ray can barely keep his eyes open. George quotes: *No more staff to help souls and put the wrong to right. The silence of the bedrooms, ghostly whispers in the hall.* The poem on the wall? Ray says. How could you know it? You were let go by then. The hospital was closed. Ben told me. George smiles. You're wrong, he says. The poem was always there, you see. On the wall. Waiting. But ... Ray says, his mind addled by the pipe smoke and this latest baffling information. It makes no sense. No sense at all. It ... He has difficulty holding up his head and it drops Raggedy-Andy heavy against his chest. His eyes slam shut and he's dead to the world.

～ The kids follow a flashlight's conical beam through the muck and clutter of the basement. They drink beer from cans. The boy is Ray, younger, in his late teens. Who's the girl? She giggles and clenches Ray's arm with the fingernails of her free hand. A rat's yellow eyes suddenly appear in front of them. The girl shrieks and giggles louder. She hunches and stamps her feet. The rat shoots away and vanishes behind some debris. Ray holds the flashlight beam upright beneath their chins, showing their faces in an eerie blue glow. He bulges his eyes, bares his teeth and makes a ghost sound. The girl slaps his shoulder and tells him to stop. She's Linda Romanchuk. Not particularly attractive: gangly, flat-chested with stringy hair, pointed nose, pinched cheeks and buckteeth. A good-time party girl who's rumoured to specialize in blowjobs so that she'd be accepted by the inner circle of school friends as well as maintain her virginity—a treasure she vowed to preserve until marriage, for some undisclosed reason. The pair are likely bombed out of their skulls or close to it. Chilly and damp, a light fog exits their mouths. They spark cigarettes, shiver, fall over each other and giggle for no reason. They both wear lightweight jackets. It's fall. Did they decide on this adventure earlier? Get liquored up and make a late-night visit to the Asylum for kicks? Or were they at a party and got bored? Decided to seek out other excitement. Ray has four beer cans hanging from his waist, his belt looped through the plastic ring. Linda grabs Ray by the chin for a kiss. She drives her tongue into his mouth for a taste of French and he repays in kind. They pull apart and laugh. C'mon, she says.

They stumble onward. She appears to be leading the way. There it is. She takes a final quick puff and ejects her butt into the darkness. I've seen it, Ray says. It's an old electric chair. Linda jumps onto the seat, grips the handles and acts like she's being electrocuted, clenching her teeth, moaning, disfiguring her face and writhing, then suddenly collapsing as if passed out. Or expired. Ray inches closer. Linda? he whispers. She pops her eyes and mouth open, leaps from the chair and laughs hysterically, slapping her knees. Ray joins in. Bitch, he says. You scared the shit out of me.

No more the cries and silent screams to echo in the night! Linda moans the words in a spooky voice straight out of a low-budget Grade B horror film.

They push and grab at each other's bodies and drink from the cans. Linda takes a small plastic bag from her coat pocket and drops a couple of pills in her hand. Take, she says. What? Ray asks. Never mind, she says. Take! She sticks out her tongue and Ray does the same. She puts a pill on each tongue. The two close their mouths and swallow.

Get in, she says, and shoves him toward the chair. Hey! No, I'd rather not. What are ya, chicken? Get in! Buk-buk-buk! Chicken! Buk-buk-buk. She pushes harder. Ray braces himself on the armrests to keep from sitting. Linda leans her weight on him, but he doesn't budge. He's stronger than her. She switches tactics. Goes all soft and talks baby-talk to him. You want mommy to give you a nice little blowjob, yeah? She lays a palm on his crotch and rubs. While you're high? Sure, you do. There's nothin' better. So, be a good little boy and do as mommy says. Ray's body sags and his head reels. Whatever drug he's been given hits him hard. His body goes all liquidly-limp and his knees cave. Linda shrieks and gives him a final firm shove. She uses the metal cuffs and leather cords to strap him in. No, Ray protests meekly, but he's unable to resist; he's barely able to raise a finger or flex a muscle. He can feel Linda fiddling with the zipper of his jeans. The flashlight drops from his limp hand and the beam goes out when it hits the floor. There's a second of darkness, then instantly, the space around him and the chair is enveloped in a sinister luminescence, as though someone has flicked on an overhead lamp. From somewhere outside the bright halo, within the shadows, he hears the mumble of disembodied voices drawing near. Where's Linda? he thinks. Is she doing this? Is she playing some kind of bizarre head game with him? Trying to fuck with his mind? Well, she's doing a pretty good job. He no longer feels her palm rubbing his crotch. Is she still in the room or what?

His head lolls as he attempts to search the area through slit eyes. All at once, a tight group of large, burly, faceless men emerge from the darkness and into the light. Some are dressed in white lab coats and pants; the rest are in tattered work clothes or rags. They surround and hover over him. They tell him not to struggle. If he struggles, they say, it'll only make things worse. They lean in. He can smell their foul sweaty flesh, their hot rancid breath. It's a reek that's seems more dead than alive. Their hands travel his body, caressing, poking, probing. The men unzip their pants and reveal immense erect cocks. Ray clenches his face. Tears squeeze down his cheeks. He's nauseous and close to vomiting but doesn't want to open his mouth. Not even to scream. He's too afraid. He tells himself that it can't be real, that it's a dream he'll soon wake from. But he doesn't wake, and the men are fumbling with his belt and undoing his pants. He attempts to struggle against the straps that hold him. It's impossible. He lacks the strength. There's nothing he can do to escape or defend himself. He decides the only possible alternative is to give in to the men's treatment of him physically while removing himself mentally from the scene by thinking of something else. Something pleasant. It's a ploy he's used in the past with some success, though not since he was a kid, and not for anything as horrific as this. But what? What image is powerful enough to transport him away from his present grim situation? He takes a deep breath through his nose, grits his teeth and presses his eyelids shut. He concentrates. Soon, a vague swirling mass begins to materialize within his mind, and he allows it, unsure, believing that anything he can lock onto and lose himself in will be miles better than his current situation. He focuses as the mass slowly takes shape, delineates itself, and becomes the clear image of a boy scout clad in short, baggy khaki knickers, canvas leggings, a khaki shirt with badges pinned on a pocket, and a red bandana knotted at the throat. He wears a paper bag over his head and salutes with two fingers.

No, Ray mutters. No, not that.

〜 "Ray makes an interesting point," Beth says. "I mean, how can you believe anything anyone tells you? Unless you were there. Even then. What is it they say? There are three sides to every story: yours, mine and the truth."

"Who says that?" Ben fills the dishwasher.

"I don't know. They. Them. I read it somewhere. Or heard it. Doesn't matter. Makes sense. Which leaves Ray. I mean, what the hell?"

"What?"

"How can you believe anything he says? He never laid a hand on Suzanne? Ha! Really? I mean, if he showed up at her place ..." Beth rolls her hands, palms up, palms down, in the air. "C'mon, this is Ray we're talking about. You don't think he isn't going to ... I mean, take advantage of the situation? Especially after what Barry did to him?"

"His point exactly. He doesn't have to do anything. People will always assume the worst."

Beth pours the remainder of Ben's wine glass into her own. "You're done with this, right?" She drinks. "The best predictor of future behaviour is past behaviour. And in Ray's case ... y'know? Just sayin'." She passes Ben a greasy platter. "Down the side, I think," and points to the dishwasher rack.

"Is that, like, Dr. Phil?

"Walter Mischel actually. Though I heard it on Dr. Phil,

so what? Besides, there've been plenty of studies to show that the maxim is highly reliable. It's used by health professionals with diagnoses and such. Even criminal behaviour, as you should know, being in law enforcement. 'Round up the usual suspects,' right? Otherwise, you might as well flip a fucking coin."

"Sometimes it comes down to trust."

"Remember that next time the fox is in the hen house."

"We don't have a hen house."

"Yeah, good thing, too. 'Cause there'd be no hens and a very fat fox picking his teeth in a corner with a chicken bone."

"You'd rather I go in guns blazing?"

"I'm just saying: recognize what's in front of you. Don't be blinded because Ray's family. You don't owe him anything, except to be fair. Treat him like everyone else."

"Except ... Ray isn't everyone else."

Beth shrugs and gives Ben a pitiful look. "You're hopeless."

"Maybe."

Beth sticks out a clenched hand, like she's holding something between her thumb and forefinger, and gives it a half twist.

"What's that?"

"That's me locking the door to the hen house. Just in case."

"You're funny."

"I'm a full-on, one-person, national riot. Speaking of which ..." She slices the air with her arm. "Mickey Mouse is taking Minnie to court. The trial goes on and on. Finally, the judge says to Mickey: I'm sorry, but I can't find any proof to your claim that Minnie is crazy. Mickey says: Judge, I never said she was crazy, I said she was fucking Goofy!" She lets out a whoop and snorts. She doubles over and slaps her knee.

Ben watches and smiles. He gets a kick out of her, even if he's not so much into her particular brand of humour. Beth downs the wine, gives the glass a rinse in the sink, then wraps her arms around Ben's waist.

"C'mon my big handsome serious trusting man. Let's kiss the kids good-night and scoot off to bed. I'm beat."

Ben closes the door to the dishwasher, flicks the lock lever and presses the on button.

"Sure," he says. "Let's go."

The couple march hand in hand through the kitchen, toward the dining room.

"Walter Mischel also developed something called the marshmallow test. Also called delayed gratification. Very interesting. Wanna hear?"

"Do I have a choice?"

"Not really."

"You sure I wouldn't appreciate hearing it more if you delayed telling me?"

"Very clever, mister! Very clever. I'll give that some thought while we check on the kids."

They open the bedroom door, peek inside and tiptoe toward the bunk beds.

〜 It's already bright and warm, the sun barely above the horizon. Ray flops his head side to side, still groggy. His body feels like it's half-buried in the earth. Turns out, it is. He's lying face-up in the soft dirt on the riverbank. He manages to lift his eyelids enough to catch a chocolate brown

Labrador sniffing his private parts. A voice hisses. Stop it, Charlie. Get away! There's the silhouette of a man bent over Ray. His hands clapped to his thighs. The man's dressed in jogging gear. He's admiring Ray's tats. One's a circle of barbed wire centred by a bleeding heart on his left bicep. A large colourful dragon winds around the right bicep. Beneath the dragon is the Chinese character script that means dragon. Another tat over his heart is the figure of a naked woman, representing Virgo, also with a script character inked beneath. The final image is that of a small red rose engraved on one shoulder. They each tell a story that is Ray. Or represents Ray. Or hints at Ray.

Are you okay? the man asks. A woman enters Ray's field of vision. She drops scraps of clothes on his exposed crotch. You might want to get into these, she says. I found them scattered. I assume they're yours. No underwear. Whether lost, or ...? She shrugs and smiles a dirty smile. Cops are on the way. Must've been quite the party. She eyes him up and down. Nice tats, she says. I've got one of a cat. Guess where?

The man and woman are likely a couple. Early thirties. Cool, calm and collected, like it's no big deal discovering a sleeping naked man on a beach. Is he okay? she asks the man. Appears to be. Probably just one too many, he says. Or three or four, she jokes. They jostle each other and laugh. Ray slowly raises himself to sitting position and crawls into his clothes. Ben arrives with a second officer in tow, and they haul Ray into the squad car.

"Is this necessary?" he asks.

"Yeah," Ben says. "It is." He tells the officer, "You take him, I'll follow behind."

At the station, they give him coffee and a bagel. He drinks the coffee. The second officer stands around, realizes he's not needed or wanted and ambles reluctantly out the door. He would've liked to see how it's handled, though he can guess.

"What happened?" Ben asks. They're sitting in his office.

"Not sure. I went to the house, like I said I would. Door was open. There was an old guy living there. Native. Cree maybe. Said his name was George Kiche. Said he'd worked with dad at the hospital. Knew our grandparents, too, apparently. Said he had the *OK* to be there."

"I never heard of him. And so far as I'm aware, no one's living in the house. It's been deserted since dad left. That said, I'll investigate personally and see if anyone's squatting. I'll also do a background check on anyone named George Kiche."

"Weird, huh?"

"Yeah. Anything else you recall?"

"We smoked a pipe. He hinted there was something stronger in it besides tobacco, but I didn't realize how much, until, *pow*! I guess I fell asleep—or passed out—shortly thereafter. Next thing I know, it's morning and I'm waking up on the shore with a dog sniffing my balls." Ray grins.

"How'd you get yourself to the beach?"

"No idea. Was my bike anywhere around?"

"Yeah, with the keys in the ignition."

"Huh. Anyway, that's the story. What's next? Can I go get my bike?"

"Not immediately. Your bike's in the parking lot. It's fine. I drove it in. Nice set of wheels. Anyway, there's a couple of things we need to discuss. Number one, I have to write you up for nude sunbathing at a public beach. There was a complaint."

"You're kidding? Not the couple with the Lab. They seemed fine. Not a big deal."

"No, there was another passer-by who wanted you charged with indecent exposure, but decided to let it go, after I explained they'd have to come into the precinct and make a statement and file an official complaint and appear in court as a material witness and so on and so forth. Seems the process was more bother than their desire to fulfill their civic duty. You're lucky you weren't discovered by any young kids, though, otherwise it coulda been worse. A lot worse. As it is, the report I file will read you had a few too many drinks and decided to crash at the beach rather than drive home. You don't know how you lost your clothes. Brownie points for acting socially responsible. No biggie—aside from the nude part—so long as it doesn't happen again. You get off with a stern warning. *Capiche*?"

"Sure, Ben. Thanks."

Ben taps the eraser end of a pencil on his desk. "Anything else you remember?"

"Such as?"

"Such as how or why you ended up at that particular location on the riverbank?" Ben gives Ray a second to respond. Ray shakes his head, no. "You were lying maybe twenty feet from where mom's shoes and blouse were discovered. The place where she most likely entered the river. Were you aware?"

"Shit, Ben. I'd totally forgotten. You sure?"

"Yeah, I'm sure." Ben drops the pencil and wipes his

hands. "Anyway, as I said, no biggie. I should probably get busy."

"Sure." Ray slouches forward in his chair. "You'll let me know what happens after you check out the house."

"No problem. I'll maybe bump into you sometime later in the day. If you're at the Detour, we'll talk. Your keys are on the hook over there. Leather jacket with sunglasses tucked in the pocket, hung on the rack beside."

Ben indicates the wall behind Ray. He watches Ray get up, grab the jacket and keys, and make his way out the door and down the hall.

The second officer wanders in and stares at Ben.

"Something on your mind, Dave?"

"Nope. Not really."

"Good." Ben picks up his pencil and pushes at a few loose sheets of paper on his desk. Without looking up, he says, "When you leave, make sure you shut the door behind you."

"Sure, Ben. Sure. Got it." Dave shuts the door with a barely audible click.

~ Beth works up a sweat in the garage, doing reps on Ben's Bowflex home gym. The boom box is cranked—Lucinda Williams wailing out *The Ghosts of Highway 20*—she's reclined at an angle against the backboard with her hands in the grips, her feet planted on either side of the bench, hauling on the tension cords. She grimaces at each rep and squints to keep the salty perspiration out of her eyes. That's right, she says. Burn it off. Her T-shirt and shorts are soaked, and she feels a warm puddle form under her lower back. At the final rep she releases the grips and rolls forward into sitting position, puffing, her elbows on her thighs. For no particular or definite reason, except maybe an intuition, a premonition, she tilts her chin and aims her vision straight ahead. There's the blurry haloed silhouette of a figure standing motionless in the garage entrance. She squints her eyes trying for a better focus. She makes out it's a man, seemingly naked, except for a headband with a feather sticking out the back. There's a white sheen to his face, like it's covered in paint, or powder.

"Who's there? Who are you?" she calls. She tries to blink the salt-burn from her eyes. She rubs with her fingertips.

The man doesn't answer, simply races forward, closes ground in a flash, reaches out his hands and arms and pins Beth's shoulders to the bench before she has a chance to react. She attempts to fight him off, but he's already straddled her body and planted his weight on the hollow of her stomach, trapping her. She lashes out with her fists. He grabs her by the wrists, holds them together with one strong hand, uses his other hand to wrap her wrists with a skipping rope and tie them tightly to a horizontal metal bar on the machine above her head. He slides his body lower down hers, all the while keeping his weight firmly centred to prevent her from further squirming and kicking.

"I'll scream, I swear," she says.

The man snags a roll of duct tape from a shelf close to the Blowflex, tears a strip and stretches it across her mouth. He does the same over her eyes. Beth yanks and twists at the skipping rope with little result, her wrists are bound so securely. The man cups a hand and applies a vice-grip around her throat. He jams her head against the backboard and squeezes. Her chest heaves as she makes a few choking sounds. She can barely breathe. She can feel her head swell with blood to the point she's afraid it might explode. The strength goes out of her arms, and she feels faint. There's nothing but blackness in her thoughts and emptiness in her body, as if her life force is draining out of her. This is it, she thinks. The will to fight has vanished. Her chin drops and her body goes limp. There's nothing more to be done.

Sensing Beth's weakened condition, the man eases the grip on her neck, rolls off of her, yanks her loose-fitting shorts down her legs past her sneakers with his free hand. She's not wearing underwear. Better. Easier. He grabs her ankles roughly and spreads her legs apart on either side of the bench. He still has her by the throat, in case. He places his other hand on her inner thigh and strokes her flesh gently. He explores her pubic hair and labia with his fingertips.

Beth lays there, unmoving, waiting.

6.

Reality's for people who can't handle drugs.

The Detour is its usual busy place for Happy Hour. Ray spots the kid at the bar and wanders on over to say hello, for the hell of it.

"Waitin' for the girlfriend?" Rays props a forearm on the brass trim of the bar.

"What?" The kid's into his cups again, already two sheets to the wind, working toward three at a steady pace. "Oh, yeah, it's you! Yeah. No. Her. No. We split up."

"That was short and sweet. Or maybe not so sweet? What happened?"

"She caught me bangin' her best friend. Tossed me out on my ass."

"Ouch! That's gotta hurt."

"Fuckin' *A*. She had a nice apartment, too. Plants and everything."

"Uh-huh." Ray wonders at the plant comment and what it might mean to the kid, on any personal level. He's got nothing and lets it go. "So, where ya stayin' now?"

"Oh, you know, her best friend took me in. Said she couldn't leave me homeless since it was mainly her fault and all. Which is what it was."

"How so?"

"Bitch came on to me. Right there in her best friend's place if you can believe. Said she was there to pick up a CD. Right. And I'm the king of whatever. One thing leads to another. Next thing I ..." He bangs a fist against his palm. "Y'know? What was I supposed to do? I'm only human, right?"

Ray gives the kid the once over. Five foot ten in work boots, skinny, bad skin, big nose. A drunk at twenty-one. He can't figure what the women see. Of course, he hasn't met the women. They may not be any great shakes either.

"I guess," he says. "And the girlfriend walked in?"

"Yeah. I was just goin' in for seconds. That'll teach me. Next time. Git 'er done and kick the bitch out before there's trouble." He smirks and taps a finger to his temple.

"Lesson learned."

"Got that right. Her place—the best friend or former best friend, I guess, it's confusing—is over a Chinese restaurant. Stinks like burnt oil and deep-fried dumplings. And she owns a cat. I'm allergic to cats. Fucking nightmare."

"Sounds tough. At least you have a roof."

"Yeah." He drinks. "You got a girlfriend or a wife?"

"No. I'm taking a sabbatical."

"You're religious?" The kid gapes.

"Sort of."

"Huh. Women, right? Can't live with 'em, can't fucking shoot 'em." The kid chuckles, clenches his eyes and gives his head a shake. "I'm a bit wasted."

"Yeah." Rays slaps the kid's shoulder. "Take care."

He finds a table to sit at. Ben walks through the front

door, catches his glance and joins him. He folds his hands on the table.

"You wouldn't believe," he says.

"Give it to me."

"I get to the house; the place is locked up tight as a drum. I use the key to go inside and it's like I said, not touched in years, dust and cobwebs everywhere. No sign of habitation, native or otherwise. No peace pipe. No potted daisies."

"C'mon Ben ... Are you shitting me? I wanna say that's impossible. I was there."

"Uh-huh. And this character George Kiche? I did a search, Ray. He was an inmate in the hospital, didn't work there. Declared certifiably insane. Apparently lobotomized in the early days as he was considered psychotic and dangerous. Murdered someone and raped someone else in a botched robbery attempt. Claimed there were voices in his head that drove him to it. The devil and so on. Died there in 2001, aged 73. Pneumonia. Right before the place shut down and dad got let go. They likely knew each other, but ..." Ben unfolds and folds his hands and rubs his thumbs together. "He's dead."

"How can that be? I saw him. I spoke with the man!"

"I gotta ask you, Ray. Are you in the habit of doing illicit drugs? I mean heavily, not the occasional toke? Or are you or have you ever been on prescription meds of any kind that can cause, say, hallucinations?" Ray grunts in the negative. "Do you have a history of blackouts, or have you ever been told you've blacked out? Apart from the episode recently. I mean, you could have dreamed this, yes? When you were on the beach passed out? Maybe dad mentioned something about the man, and gave his name at some point, and you created this story in your head about meeting him at the house?"

"No, Ben. No hallucinations. There's just the dreams. And this seemed different. It seemed real. And it was broad daylight. I was awake."

"Uh-huh. And do you happen to know what the name 'Kiche' means in Cree?"

"Not a clue."

"It means 'spirit.'"

"Shit Ben. Are you saying I'm talking to ghosts?"

"No. I'm saying the mind's a funny thing. Maybe you should see a doctor."

"You mean a shrink."

"I mean a doctor. Start there, see what they say. I can give you a name."

A waitress floats by. "Sorry boys, for making you wait. We just changed shifts. What can I do you for? Though I guess you're on duty, right Ben?"

Ben nods and gives his chin a scratch.

"Pint of whatever's the special," Ray says. The waitress leaves. "Give me the doctor's name Ben. I'll make an appointment. I promise." Ray stares at Ben who doesn't drop his gaze. "Something else?"

"Yeah. You lied to me, Ray. About Suzanne. You said you never laid a finger on her. A neighbour saw you drive up to her place on your bike. Saw you go inside the house. You were in there a while."

"I didn't lie to you, Ben. Yeah, I went in the house for a beer, and we talked. Beyond that, it's what I said. I never laid a finger on her. I went to her place to apologize for my bad behaviour years ago and that's what I did. She accepted my apology. I left. That was it. Nothing else happened."

"But you see what it looks like."

"I can't help what it looks like, Ben. I've told you my side of the story. Check with Suzanne and see what she says."

"You make it hard for me, Ray. In my position."

"Sorry, Ben. It can't be easy being a sheriff and my brother. All I ask is, check it out."

"I'll do that. You know I will. As a matter of course. Because it *is* my job, like it or not. However" —Ben rises from his chair—"we both know there's no way of proving whether she'll be telling me the truth or spinning tales, is there? I mean, if something did happen between the two of you, she has every reason to lie."

Ray clicks his tongue and leans back in his chair. "Life's a shit sandwich, right Ben? You remember."

"And every day you have to take another bite. I know."

"I think it was Dr. Phil who said that. Or maybe Mother Teresa. I get the two confused, sometimes."

Ben says his good-byes and hits the street. Ray reaches down, inches a cell phone from the back of a boot and holds it hidden under the table, between his thighs. He hits the screen and types in a question. He goes to a link explaining that canvas leggings for Boy Scout uniforms were dropped in 1923, replaced by knee socks.

Sonofabitch, thinks Ray. That's even before grandpa's time. He slides the cell into the boot. Guess I'll need to pay dad another visit. See about that other book. If there is another book.

〜 There's some of the regular crowd shooting pool, drinking beer, generally horsing around. Ray joins them. They're a few years younger than him. All either single and working or married with kids and working. The conversation is casual and moves easily from topic to topic. Somehow the subject of Weyburn is raised.

"To Weyburn, the city of opportunity," Ray quotes, holding up his pint. "Just look around and witness the evidence in all its glory." Everyone laughs. Huh, he thinks. They're enjoying themselves and oblivious to the touch of sarcasm in his voice, the dig. Or maybe he only thinks he's being sarcastic. Or maybe he's softened, lost his touch. Or maybe it's an old joke between the locals and they've all heard it before and no one gives a good goddamn. Or maybe they're really that stupid that they don't know when they and their empty little bovine lives are being ridiculed. Whatever. Seems he can't be sure of anything anymore.

"What about you, Ray? You lookin' for work? There's job openings at Souris River Seeds, or else in construction. Plenty of building going on these days. Anyone who can swing a hammer."

"Ray don't need to work." A cute young gal cosies up to Ray and rubs a hand provocatively up and down a pool cue tip. "Do you, Ray? I heard you got money stashed away in a suitcase up at the trailer. Made it from selling refrigerators to Eskimos."

General laughter. They're making it up as they go along. Nothing insincere, no animosity, no 'malice aforethought.'

"I heard he made it in real estate." This is the boyfriend of the gal. Used to be the class clown in high school, now he's a grease monkey at a neighbourhood garage and gas bar. "Buy high, sell low. How does he do it? Volume. Har-har ..."

"Nothing in my suitcase except dirty laundry," Ray says. "Feel free to come on over anytime and take a sniff."

They're good kids, thinks Ray. They're happy. Everything slides off them like Teflon. Must be nice. All well and good until someone loses an eye. Makes me want to puke. Makes me want to grab the cute gal by the snatch and fucking dig in my nails. Smash her boyfriend's face to a pulp with a cue ball. Bust a chair over someone's head. Why is that? Because they don't know, that's why. They haven't been through it. The initiation. The drill. I want to say: What the fuck do you know? What the fuck are you laughing about, limp dicks and cock sucking bitches? You don't know! You don't have a fucking clue what's out there; what it's all about. The fucking horror.

Ray's about to explode and go ape shit on the room when Suzanne's truck driving husband Donnie comes charging across the floor, raging like a man on fire.

"Motherfucker!" he screams. "I'll kill you, motherfucker!"

Something clicks in Ray's head. Is it live or is it Memorex? After that, it's a blur. Fists fly, furniture smashes, blows are exchanged. Eventually, quickly—almost immediately—bodies are wrenched apart. It's over in seconds. Donnie lies on his back on the floor bleeding from his cheek and lip. Bleeding, but breathing. His limbs jerkily flexing and twisting in some insect-like manner. Ray is on his knees, also bleeding. A slight cut over the eye, some superficial cuts on the hands. From a busted bottle or beer glass, he suspects. He's lifted bodily and ushered unceremoniously out of the bar by a couple of panicked staff.

"Shit, Ray," they say. "Shit! Get outta here."

I'm innocent, thinks Ray. It was self-defence. I had no choice. He came at me. Fucking Donnie. It was me or him.

Cocksucker. Motherfucker.

Awkward hands toss him on his bike and sit him up straight. Someone turns the key in the ignition.

"For chrissakes, Ray," voices mumble. "Get the fuck outta here before the cops come."

Ray kicks it and guns the engine. He pops the clutch and tears on out.

That turned out fine, he thinks. I feel better. Calmer. Managed to let off steam and it wasn't my fault. Fucking Donnie. Right on! Lots of witnesses. He came at me. I had no choice in the matter. It was self-defence. Ray laughs and takes a deep breath. Good. I feel good. And I have Donnie to thank. Who'd've thought? Fucking Donnie. Comes at me like a raging maniac in my hour of need. Funny. Okay. Thanks Donnie! Thank you. I can relax for a while. Get my head clear. Think about other things. It's all good.

⌁ The sun takes its own sweet time setting, though Ben knows, now that it's hit the horizon, it'll quickly sink and vanish, leaving nothing except a red-orangey afterglow. He's plunked in the dirt on the bank of the river, his knees bent to his chest, his feet spread apart in front of him. He's dressed in shorts and flip-flops, shirtless, sunglasses pushed on top of his head. He's got a six-pack of beer next to him, four cans being empty and crushed. He drinks from a fifth, while the sixth waits its turn, still attached to the plastic harness. Between his feet sit a pair of women's shoes—plain-looking, scuffed brown leather, low heels, worn straps—and, alongside, a lightweight faded-white cotton blouse. He picks the blouse off the ground, crushes it in his palm, holds it to his face and rubs it forcibly against his cheek. He gives the blouse a sniff, a kiss, and sets it gently back down. He pokes and caresses the shoes. He uses two fingers to lift one shoe by the strap and hold it up for inspection. He turns it in the air. His chest heaves slightly, he swallows attempting to quash a hiccup, but the breath escapes. His body trembles and a soft moan exits his mouth. He sucks air through his teeth, clenches his eyes, and weeps softly. He wipes the tears with the heel of a hand. He raises the beer can to his lips, throws back his head, drains the contents, crushes the can, and drops it with the others. He rubs and massages his scalp and gives his nose a tug. He places one shoe beside the other, slips his hands inside and walks them back and forth, heel to toe. He turns one shoe inward, tilts it to the side and returns it flat to the ground. He removes his hands and carefully folds the blouse on top of the shoes.

He unharnesses the last beer, pops the tab, and drinks. He stares at the river's edge, watches a dragonfly hover above a damp log. He remains situated in this position, his body dissolving to shadow as the light fades and finally disappears altogether.

～ The bonfire's ablaze when Ray reaches the camper trailer. He hits the brakes; the bike's rear tire skids forward and he donuts to a stop. There's a bulging yellow moon. Beneath it, within the glow, he sees Tantoo. She's dressed in full ceremonial garb, replete with feathered headdress, beaded blouse, decorated buckskin skirt and snakeskin boots. She dances around the flames, alternately howling and chanting at whatever gods might be listening. In the distant hills, coyotes and wolves yip and yowl along with her.

Ray staggers over to greet her. She displays little alarm at his battered appearance, simply grins and *tut-tuts* with her tongue, like: what, again? Ah, well.

She swipes at the caking blood over his eye with a thumb, contents herself there's no real serious damage and offers him the pipe. He inhales several puffs in rapid succession. He tosses his head and lets it rip, a wailful howl at the sky. Tantoo returns to her dance and describes some type of magic symbols in the air with her bent fingers. Ray is still at a total loss to understand what they represent or what she's attempting to communicate, if indeed, she is attempting to communicate. Random, he thinks. Improvised. Meaningless. Except to her? Okay. Fine. Whatever. All at once, he can barely remain standing, never mind concentrate. His arms wander the area around his body in no particular pattern, like a man floating underwater. I'm wasted, he tells her. He mimes drinking a beer and makes a drunken face. I'm going inside. He points. *Inside*. He stumbles in the direction of the trailer, hauls himself up the two steps, gropes his way to his room and throws himself on the mattress. It's as if his body's filled with wispy blue smoke. Which surprises him because—as he's so fond of telling himself—he never gets drunk, so, what's happening? What's happened? Of course, the pipe.

He's drifting, unsure if he's asleep or awake or only dreams he's awake.

He remains half-aware. There's some kind of a commotion going on outside the trailer. The sounds of vehicles pulling up. SUV and truck engines throb. Through the curtains, the sweep of headlights and spotlights pulse from super-charged batteries. He imagines coolers of beer spilling from lowered tailgates as retro music blasts full-throttle from high-end speakers—*Psycho Killer*, by Talking Heads, *Because the Night*, by Patti Smith—youthful voices sing along, shout: Hey, Ray! Ray! Ray! they chant. C'mon out, man! Have a beer with us! Join us! There's BBQ happening.

What else? Bonfires dotting the landscape. Visions of young, attractive, scantily clad, enormously breasted women wearing Stetson hats dancing slo-mo on vehicle roofs. Some-one who looks vaguely like George Kiche, his face done up in white war paint, gyrating along with them. The entire scene resembles a grainy vintage MuchMusic video or something out of a David Lynch film. At any moment Ray expects to hear the voice of Dennis Hopper say: sing *Candy Coloured Clown*.

He's in a fog. His brain only partially functional, his body seeming less so. What the fuck? he thinks. There's a weight bouncing and grinding on his mid-section. He is somewhat aware that he has managed to attain an erection and is involved in sexual intercourse. His hands seem to be latched onto a pair of skinny bony rocking buttocks. He fights to open his eyes and gaze upward. There's a naked woman on top of him, moaning pleasurably, her back and neck arched, her pelvis thrusting. Long jet-black hair streaked with grey drapes her shoulders. Her exposed breasts are small and withered. Ray diverts his eyes so as to travel past the woman's saggy haunch to the right ankle. He's able to distinguish a tattoo—a circle of turtles. No! he cries. No! He sweeps the woman aside with an arm and scrambles out of bed. The woman bounces across the floor and lands hard, smashing into a side table. The table leg snaps and a ceramic lamp crashes down on the woman's head and shatters. It's Tantoo. She stretches her arms out to him and flexes her hands, imploringly. There's a bloody cut above her eye. Ray tucks himself into his pants and buckles his belt. From outside he hears the continuing chant: Ray! Ray! Ray! He opens the door and is met by a barrage of headlights, spotlights, and even tactical hunting flashlights. The music blares louder. Bonfires roar. He crosses his arms in front of his face in order to shade his eyes so he can locate his bike. When he does find it, he clambers aboard and roars through the crowd, onto the dirt road and deep into the prairie night.

In his head, the steady din of Ray! Ray! Ray! reverberates and lingers.

〜 There's a light in the shack window and smoke rising from the chimney. Ray wonders what his dad might be doing up this time of night. Though, who knows, maybe the man doesn't sleep, wouldn't surprise him.

The door's unlocked and slightly ajar. Ray doesn't knock, doesn't announce himself, just nudges the handle and marches in. His dad sits in a rocker, his back to him, facing the roaring fire. Seems to be a night for fire and bright lights, thinks Ray. His dad twists his scrawny neck. He wears a mad grin stretched ear to ear.

"I knew you'd be back, Ray. I been waitin' for ya."

"That a fact? Then you know what I'm lookin' for."

Ray steps toward his dad who springs out of the chair. For an old man, he's quick and agile. He raises a hand in the air. It holds a black hard-covered journal.

"You made me a promise last time. You didn't keep it."

"It was the wrong book."

"You didn't know that."

"I know it now. I want the real one."

"Too late, Ray. Shoulda kept your word. I left you a note where to find it, earlier. If you'd done what you promised. Now, it's too late."

His dad tosses the journal into the fire. Ray makes a leap to retrieve it from the flames. The old man blocks his way and tears at Ray's eyes with his fingernails. He's strong, stronger than one would think or expect; he gouges deeper. Ray secures his dad's wrists and rips them away. His dad twists and kicks and Ray shoves him flailing into the chair. Ray reaches for the journal. He can't grab hold of it; the fire's too hot. He tries to stab at it with a finger to push it off the burning logs and away from the flames. His dad attacks again and drags Ray backward by the collar. Ray snatches a metal poker from a holder on the hearth, separates himself from his dad, and proceeds to slash at the old man's arms and shoulders, finally bashing him twice in the head, cracking his skull. His dad wobbles for an instant, drops his arms, then crumples to the floor.

He lays there, motionless.

Ray takes a sidelong glance at the journal, consumed by the fire. The final pages char and curl to ash. He looks again at his dad, who still doesn't budge. Ray releases the poker. He blinks several times and rubs blood from his eyes with his jacket sleeve. He's almost blind. He feels his way out of the house using the furniture as support. Beneath the moon, he can just make out the location and shape of his Triumph. Once on the highway, he tries to figure out his next move. He's headed south, he thinks. From reflex more than anything. Weyburn's out. US border through Oungre is closed until the morning, so that's out as well. In the meantime, someone'll be looking for him. Trying to bring him back. Ben, for sure. There's been too much commotion to ignore.

He cranks the accelerator and crouches his chin between the handlebars. He stares across the top of the headlight as it illuminates the way along the empty road. Suddenly, a man emerges from the gravel shoulder and plunges himself onto the middle of the road. He turns and begins to dance within the cone of light. His face is painted white. Ray has no choice but to swerve to avoid him. He loses control. The bike leans, the wheels go out from under, the bike topples and spins. Ray is thrown from the seat and sent rolling into a mix of bush, buffalo grass, fence post and barbed wire. He bangs his head on the post. The bike flies off in the opposite direction.

Before he loses consciousness completely, he's able to catch a final glimpse of the highway. On it, beneath the dull glow of the moon, he spots the faint outline of the man, still dancing. He appears to be naked and wears a headband with a feather at the back. He covers his mouth with a palm and whoops. He tosses his head, arches his back and howls into the night. The coyotes howl in response.

〰 Ben's settled in an armchair near the bed when Ray comes to, alerted by a growly moan.

"Hey, bud." Ben vacates the chair in one easy movement and huddles in close. He lays a hand on Ray's shoulder.

"Ben?"

"Yeah."

"I can't see." Bandages cover Ray's eyes. "What's the damage?"

"You lost control of your motorcycle. Bike's a write-off. You came out slightly better. You've been in hospital unconscious for three days. Banged your head pretty bad. Also, some injury to your eyes, but the doc figures you'll be okay. Bandages come off today and she'll know better." Ben turns his attention to the door as two people in white uniforms enter the room, the doctor and a nurse. "Speak of the devil."

"How's our patient?" the doctor asks.

"Alive and kicking," Ben says.

Ben steps away to allow the doctor and nurse space.

"Is that true?"

"What he said," Ray says. "Takes a licking, goes on ticking."

"Good. I'm going to remove the bandages. We'll close off most of the light in the room so you can adjust slowly, okay? Nurse."

The nurse dims the room. The doctor makes a few quick cuts and drops the soiled bandages and pads onto a metal tray. "Take your time opening," she says. "No hurry. Any pain?"

"No pain. Feels like cotton batten is still there. So far, so good. A bit blurry, but I can make out shapes." He raises his eyelids fully and blinks a couple of times. "Seems fine. Everything's grey. Maybe we can try some light?"

The nurse bumps the slider on the light switch.

"Okay, it's good. I can see. How are things otherwise? Still in possession of all my parts? Anything missing or broken?"

"You're a lucky man. Not exactly miracle material, but close. Bashed, battered, and bruised. A nasty bump on the skull. You had some episodes of delirium, perhaps even hallucinations while you were unconscious. Likely due to the trauma. That's it. Of course, to be sure, we'll run some more tests before you leave." She checks her cell. "I'm needed elsewhere. I'll leave you with your brother, now. You likely want to talk."

Ben and Ray wait until the doctor and nurse exit.

"Hallucinations, huh? Such as?"

"All variety of stuff. Mostly, you were going on and on that Tantoo was our mother; that she bore the identifying mark of a circle of turtles tattooed around her right ankle. You said something about needing to find a journal that dad had in his possession. It would explain everything. You went to see him. When you got to his house, he was burning the journal in the fireplace. You tried to save it, the two of you fought, and you killed him."

Ben relates the incidents in a matter-of-fact manner, with no hint of either judgement or blame.

"Christ, Ben, that's bad, and it's not even the half of it! Tantoo and I ... we had sex together. That is, I woke up and she was on top of me. Except, I didn't know she was our mother at the time. I only saw the tattoo later. I mean, we were already ... y'know? Doing it." Ray stares quizzically at Ben, who stands nodding dumbly, almost imperceptibly. "Then, there was that mob of kids outside the trailer. Raising a ruckus, cranking out tunes and dancing and chanting for me to come out. And George Kiche ... I saw him again, with the kids, dancing, and later on the highway, I think. Except he seemed different. Younger, slimmer."

"Stop it, Ray. Okay?" Ben's voice is calm, but firm. "Just stop it. And listen to yourself a minute. Listen to what you're saying." Ben can see the question mark on Ray's face and can tell he has no idea what he's getting at. Or trying to get at. Ben takes a deep breath and blows it out through his nose. "Right, okay. I need you to know, none of what you've said so far is true. None of it. Not a word. Not a goddamn thing. As far as I can tell, it was all a dream. Or, like the doctor said, a hallucination due to the conk on the noggin. I'm serious, Ray. You've got to get it together and try and figure out what's real and what isn't. You understand me?"

"Check it out, Ben. See for yourself."

"I already have. Not because I necessarily believed it, but because it's my job. To begin, while there were witnesses to Donnie coming after you in the bar—he's fine by the way, and the fight was his fault by all accounts, so you're in the clear in that department—but no one in town admits to driving into the countryside for a party at the trailer. Secondly, dad's fine. Not a scratch on him. He doesn't know anything about any journal. He doesn't know anything about a tattoo of turtles on our mother's ankle, which he says she never had. Moreover, he says he doesn't recall you ever coming to visit. I mean, ever. Not the second time, not the first time, even."

"Dad's a bit of a piss-tank. And, also, not all-together there, mentally. Wouldn't surprise me if he didn't remember. I told you, he asked me to kill him, right? He gave me a journal the first visit. Turns out it was the wrong journal and totally useless."

"What journal, Ray? Where is it? What was it about?"

"I don't know where it is. I had it at the Detour. Left it on a pile of newspapers. It was supposed to belong to our grandfather. It was supposed to give details, explain things.

Huh! Must've got tossed out with the recycle. Or the garbage. Doesn't matter since it was the wrong journal, anyway. Totally bogus. Dad burned the real one."

"Uh-huh."

"Don't look at me like that. You think I'm making this shit up? Why would I? And what about Tantoo?"

"There's nothing to tell, Ray. She's also fine and un-injured. No signs of damage to either her or the trailer. No signs of a struggle anywhere. When I arrived, she was calmly sewing together a leather moccasin."

The men sit quietly. Ben sniffs in a short breath and coughs. His intention is to parcel out the information in small chunks so Ray can easily absorb it and understand the gravity.

"Meanwhile, you told me earlier you didn't own a cell, yeah? Well, one was found in your saddlebag. The thing is —and I'm the first to admit our crime lab doesn't compare to NCIS—my people tell me the thing's broken. And it's been broken for several years, which raises the million-dollar question: What were you doing carrying around a busted cell phone?"

Ray stares vacantly across the bed. His mind is doing cartwheels. He clicks his teeth. He speaks and the words come out of his mouth like they're not his. Like they're weak and hollow.

"What's going on, Ben? What's happening to me?"

"Don't know, Ray. Are you sure you didn't simply have it out with Donnie in the bar, hop on your bike, take it for a spin, and accidentally run off the road? Nothing else in between. No kids partying, no sexual escapades with Tan-too, no knocking dad off with a metal poker, no mysterious

144

journal gone up in flames, no dancing native American George Kiche in whiteface, huh? It would make it a whole lot easier."

"Make what easier?"

Ben checks behind over his shoulder and satisfied no one's there, leans in toward Ray for a whisper.

"I gotta be honest with you, bud ... everything you've been saying, everything you've done since the day you hit town, then these most recent events, has led the doctors here in the hospital to believe you are not of sound mind. In fact, they're asking me to sign you over for psychiatric observation and possible treatment in a local institution."

Ray's face goes blank. His jaw hangs. He has difficulty forming a sentence. What sentence? The correct sentence. What correct sentence? There is no correct sentence.

"Ben," he utters. "I wouldn't last a day in one of those places, you know that."

"I know. Which is why I'm asking—listen to me—could it have happened the way I said, and the rest is all fantasy due to the concussion?"

Ray gives it a second's consideration. His brain is suddenly somehow functioning again. Fear can do that, he thinks.

"It could've, Ben. Yeah, given everything, plus the accident and bump on the skull, I could've imagined it, sure."

"Okay. That's good, Ray. I'm glad to hear that. How you feeling right now? Physically, I mean. You good? You able to move, able to see, okay?"

Ray flexes his joints and stretches his muscles. "Good, Ben. I feel good."

"Okay. The thing is, I gotta be somewhere soon. Police

business. An accident. Some kid fell off a roof doing a job and broke his neck."

"He okay?"

"Dead. Barely twenty-one. Sad."

"Mobile crane operator?"

"Yeah. Did you know him?"

"Not really. Talked with him a couple of times at the Detour. Bit of a shithead loser if you ask me. The world's better off without him."

"Uh-huh. Okay. Anyway. Before that—meaning now—I gotta go meet with the doctors and let them know I need more time to think about you and your condition. To decide what to do. It's gonna take me a few minutes with them. I'll keep 'em busy asking questions and so on and so forth, humming and hawing. Right? You'll be in the room alone. A clean set of clothes are in the closet over there. That's my jacket there on the chair." He points to each location to make sure Ray is following. "The keys to my Harley are in the right-hand pocket. The bike's parked out back, you can't miss it. It's gassed up, ready to go. The insurance slip is in the saddle-bag along with some cash. You understand what I'm saying? What I'm telling you?"

"Yeah, Ben. I understand." Ray raises a hand and the two grip palms. "S'long, little brother. Thanks."

"Yeah. Take care, Ray."

"I always do. You know that."

Ben stifles a laugh. "Yeah. Yeah. Sure, you do." He grabs his hat from the bedpost and saunters slowly out of the room and down the hall. He doesn't look back.

7.

Weyburn: the city of opportunity!

Ben's at the BBQ. He's got steaks sizzling on the grill. Beth's in the house tossing a fresh salad. There're potatoes baking in the oven and fresh asparagus ready to be steamed on the stove top. It's end of summer, still hot, and the picnic table is set for three inside the mosquito-netted gazebo. Ben's dad pulls the Buick into the drive. He's dressed in his Sunday best: starched white shirt, gray jacket and black tie, black slacks, polished black patent leather shoes.

"Pop!" Ben calls. "Good to see you. I told you, dress casual. It's BBQ."

Ben wears camouflage shorts, matching T-shirt and blue flip-flops.

"This *is* casual for Sunday, Ben. I brought a tub of ice cream. French vanilla."

Beth steps outside. She has a light blue sundress on and brown sandals. Her hair's pulled back and clipped with a butterfly barrette. Pop removes the bucket of ice cream from the paper bag.

"Hi pop," she calls, and offers everyone lemonade. Pop

hands her the bucket. She gives him a kiss on the cheek. "Ice cream, great. I'll put it in the freezer until we're ready."

"Not too long, it's better a little melted." Pop pulls the paper bag over his head and raises his arms in the air. He growls and hunches toward Ben like he's Frankenstein.

"Aaaaaarrrrrrggggghhhhh ..." he goes. Ben chuckles. "Remember when I used to do that to all the kids in the neighbourhood?"

"Yeah, when you jumped out from behind the door, you scared the living daylights out of us."

"That was the idea." He pulls the bag off, folds it and tucks it neatly into his coat pocket. "I'll reuse it."

Dinner's served on the picnic table inside the gazebo and the three sit. Beth pours wine for Ben and herself. There's an empty glass in front of Pop beside a tumbler of water. He raises a hand of refusal. Everyone knows. It's more a ritual than anything. The request goes to Pop to say grace and he obliges.

Amens all around. They dig in.

"Beth tells me you finally hired yourself a housekeeper. How's that going?"

"Should've done it years ago," Pop says, beaming. "She comes in once a week and what a difference. It's a fact. It takes a woman's touch to make a house a home. She even brought a potted plant last week. Some kind of orchid, I think. Supposed to be easy to manage. We'll see."

"That's terrific. Glad to hear it."

"Hey, have you heard this one?" Beth asks. "About a man who, deep in prayer, asks the Lord for a wish. The Lord answers him saying that, since he has been faithful, he can have his wish. The man asks for a bridge to Hawaii, but the Lord says that this is a very materialistic wish and will be difficult to grant. He asks the man to think of another wish that would honour and glorify Him. The man thinks harder and wishes instead to be able to understand women. The Lord ponders this for a moment and then replies: Do you want that bridge with two or four lanes?"

The men politely consider the joke, smile, and bob their heads somewhat hesitantly, as if considering the ramifications.

"Very nice," pop says. "Very amusing. Though perhaps somewhat cheeky, I think. It's fine among family but you might not care to repeat it to the Church congregation." He gives her a wink.

Beth shrugs, smiles, and sips her wine.

"Pop," Ben says, changing the subject. "Before I forget." He drags a journal from beside him and hands it over. "We recently found this in the possession of a young man. I'm wondering what you make of it."

Pop takes the journal and opens to the first page. He reads aloud: These are the personal notes of Frank (Francis) Nowak. Love, Vicki, 1968. P.S. Don't worry, I bought it cheap at the Church bazaar sale. Pop has a surprised look on his face.

"My goodness. I have no idea. I've never seen it before. Though, it appears to have once belonged to my father. What do you know? Of course, a lot of his stuff went off to various charities and so on after he died, but still ... To have survived and turned up now ... A young man, you say. Who?"

"Some kid who died of a broken neck in town. Funny. It was in his knapsack."

Pop flips through the pages. "Son of a gun. The rest of the journal is blank. Ha! Doesn't surprise me, though. Typical of my dad. Wasn't much of a communicator, as I recall. Whether spoken or in print."

He pushes the journal towards Beth, who opens to a page, then quickly slides it aside, to the end of the table. She rolls her eyes and shakes her head. All three laugh.

"Well," Beth says. "Strange."

"Yeah," Ben says. "That's what I thought."

They pause for a few seconds to consider. Pop breaks the silence.

"So, what's on the agenda tonight for after dinner amusement?"

"Figured we'd put *The Wild One* on the DVD player, y'know? Considering."

Beth and pop rock their heads and glance back and forth at each other, not so much uncomfortable as resigned to the decision.

Beth suddenly takes a deep breath and slaps the table with her fingers for attention. "I have some news to share," she announces. "This will be my last glass of wine for a spell."

The men regard her curiously.

"Wait! Does this mean ...?" Ben says.

"That's right. I'm pregnant."

The two men grin and applaud.

"Praise God," pop says. "It's a miracle, yes? A miracle."

"We'd begun to give up hope," Ben says. "The doctors all said ..."

"Shows what doctors know about anything, these days," pop says. "Leave it in God's hands. That's what I always say. And He, in His infinite wisdom, goodness and grace, shall provide in His time."

"Are you happy, Ben?" Beth asks.

"More than I can say, honey. It's great news. Fantastic news. I couldn't be happier. Or prouder." He leans across the table, squeezes her arm and gives her a kiss on the mouth. "I'm over the moon, really."

They continue to cut into their steaks and pass around the condiments. Compliments to the chefs are bantered about as the meat's pink flesh oozes blood. They section the potatoes and fill the openings with butter and sour cream. The salad bowl makes the rounds with a choice of dressings. A usual Sunday dinner with family becomes a meal of celebration.

"Oh," Ben says, stopping mid-bite. "And let's not forget. To Ray!" He raises his glass, and the others follow suit.

"To Ray," they say.

"He'd be twenty-nine today. May God bless his soul." Ben drinks.

"Amen to that," pop says.

"Amen." Beth wets her lips with the wine.

"His was always a troubled soul," pop continues. "There's no denying."

Beth sighs and stretches a thin smile.

"We all did our level best, God knows, We tried. Everyone tried. There wasn't any more we could do."

Pop and Beth both look at Ben who stares vacantly down at the table, then rolls his shoulders, takes a breath and returns the looks, like: *I know. It's okay, I'm fine.*

Everyone relaxes. They sip from their glasses and smile one to the other. Done with the toast, they pick up their cutlery and tuck back into their meals.

"You know how they make holy water, don't you?" Pop displays his tumbler to Ben and Beth and gives it a swirl.

"Take ordinary tap water and boil the hell out of it," they say in unison. It's an old joke that Pop never tires of telling. They all laugh and eat.

"Remember," Beth jumps in. "There's dessert. Pop brought ice cream and I baked an apple pie. Save some room."

"Amen to that," Ben says. He reaches a hand to Beth, and she takes it in her own. Their eyes are filled with joy as they gaze at each other. "Amen to that."

Beth leans in close, wraps an arm around Ben and buries her face in his neck.

Pop crawls his hand toward the journal and gently taps the cover with his fingertips. Yes, he thinks. Yes, indeed. Amen to that.

Acknowledgments

Sincere thanks to my publishers Michael Mirolla and Connie McParland, and Guernica Editions for choosing to publish this novel. Also, to my editor Sonia Di Placido whose concise comments and suggestions impelled me to re-look at my original manuscript and create something substantially better. The novel owes its germination to the Bruce Springsteen song "Highway Patrolman" followed by a viewing of the Sean Penn film *The Indian Runner* which, in turn, was based on the same Springsteen tune, so thanks to them.

The movie soundtrack (for those keeping score) includes:
Pink Houses: John Mellencamp
Big Yellow Taxi: Joni Mitchell
Glory Days: Bruce Springsteen
Stuck in the Middle with You: Stealers Wheel
Daytripper: The Beatles
Something to Talk About: Bonnie Raitt
Dry Town: Miranda Lambert
Ride of the Valkyries: Richard Wagner
The Kids Are All Right: The Who
Straight Tequila Night: John Anderson
The Ballad of Easy Rider: Roger McGuinn

Righteousness: Lucinda Williams
Powderfinger: Neil Young
It's Five O'clock Somewhere: Jimmy Buffett
The Cheapest Key: Kathleen Edwards
The Ghosts of Highway 20: Lucinda Williams
Psycho Killer: Talking Heads
Because the Night: Patti Smith
Candy Colored Clown: Roy Orbison

About the Author

Stan Rogal was born in Vancouver and now lives and writes in Toronto. He is recently retired from the University of Toronto Standardized Patient Program, where he taught and assessed communication skills for students and professionals within the health care system. His literary work has appeared in numerous magazines and anthologies in Canada, the US and Europe, some in translation. He is the author of 24 books: 5 novels, 7 story and 12 poetry collections. He is also a produced playwright.

Printed in December 2021
by Gauvin Press,
Gatineau, Québec